“Y ”
He Said Gently.

“And I’ve shown you. But this is as far as it goes. I care too much to seduce you just for an hour of pleasure.”

She swallowed, studying his hard face, her body still tingling from the touch of his fingers, her mouth warm from the long, hungry kiss they’d shared. “Should I be ashamed, Cade?” she asked.

He brushed the damp hair away from her face. “Of what?” he asked tenderly. “Of wanting to know how it felt to be touched and kissed by a man?”

She drew in a deep, slow breath. “Not . . . by a man,” she corrected. “By you.”

DIANA PALMER

is a prolific romance writer who got her start as a newspaper reporter. Accustomed to the daily deadlines of a journalist, she has no problem with writer’s block. In fact, she averages a book every two months. Mother of a young son, Diana met and married her husband within one week: “It was just like something from one of my books.”

Dear Reader,

SILHOUETTE DESIRE is an exciting new line of contemporary romances from Silhouette Books. During the past year, many Silhouette readers have written in telling us what other types of stories they'd like to read from Silhouette, and we've kept these comments and suggestions in mind in developing SILHOUETTE DESIRE.

DESIREs feature all of the elements you like to see in a romance, plus a more sensual, provocative story. So if you want to experience all the excitement, passion and joy of falling in love, then SILHOUETTE DESIRE is for you.

I hope you enjoy this book and all the wonderful stories to come from SILHOUETTE DESIRE. I'd appreciate any thoughts you'd like to share with us on new SILHOUETTE DESIRE, and I invite you to write to us at the address below:

Jane Nicholls
Silhouette Books
PO Box 177
Dunton Green
Sevenoaks
Kent
TN13 2YE

DIANA PALMER

Snow Kisses

Silhouette Desire

Published by Silhouette Books

First printing 1984

British Library C.I.P.

Palmer, Diana
Snow kisses.—(Silhouette desire)
I. Title
813′.54[F]   PS3566.A5/

ISBN 0 340 35441 0

The characters and situations in this book are entirely imaginary and bear no relation to any real person or actual happening

Printed and bound in Great Britain for Hodder and Stoughton Paperbacks, a division of Hodder and Stoughton Ltd., Mill Road, Dunton Green, Sevenoaks, Kent (Editorial Office: 47 Bedford Square, London, WC1 3DP) by Richard Clay (The Chaucer Press) Ltd., Bungay, Suffolk

Other Silhouette Books by Diana Palmer

Heather's Song
The Cowboy and the Lady
September Morning
Friends and Lovers
Fire and Ice
Darling Enemy

To the state of Montana,
whose greatest natural resource is her people.

Snow Kisses

1

The road was little more than a pair of ruts making lazy brown paths through the lush spring grass of southern Montana, and Hank was handling the truck like a tank on maneuvers. But Abby gritted her teeth and didn't say a word. Hank, in his fifty-plus years, had forgotten more about ranch work than she'd ever learn. And she wasn't about to put him in a bad temper by asking him to slow down.

She stared out over the smooth, rolling hills where Cade's white-faced Herefords grazed on new spring grass. Montana. Big Sky country. Rolling grasslands that seemed to go on forever under a canopy of blue sky. And amidst the grass, delicate yellow and blue wildflowers that Abby had gathered as a girl. Here, she could forget New York and the nightmare of the past two weeks. She could heal her wounds and hide away from the world.

She smiled faintly, a smile that didn't quite reach her pale brown eyes, and she clenched her hands around the beige purse in the lap of her shapeless dress. She didn't feel like a successful fashion model when she was on the McLaren ranch. She felt like the young girl who'd grown up in this part of rural southern Montana, on the ranch that had been absorbed by Cade's growing empire after her father's death three years earlier.

At least Melly was still there. Abby's younger sister had an enviable job as Cade's private secretary. It meant that she could be near her fiancé, Cade's ranch foreman, while she supported herself. Cade had never approved of Jesse Shane's decision to allow his eldest daughter to go to New York, and he had made no secret of it. Now Abby couldn't help wishing she'd listened. Her brief taste of fame hadn't been worth the cost.

She felt bitter. It was impossible to go back, to relive those innocent days of her youth when Cade McLaren had been the sun and moon. But she mourned for the teenager she'd been that long-ago night when he'd carried her to bed. It was a memory she'd treasured, but now it was a part of the nightmare she'd brought home from New York. She wondered with a mind numbed by pain if she'd ever be able to let any man touch her again.

She sighed, gripping the purse tighter as Hank took one rise a little fast and caused the pickup to lurch to one side. She clutched the edge of the seat as the vehicle all but rocked onto its side.

"Sorry about that," Hank muttered, bending over

the steering wheel with his thin face set into rigid lines. "Damned trucks—give me a horse any day."

She laughed softly—once she would have thrown back her head and given out a roar of hearty laughter. She might have been a willowy ghost of the girl who left Painted Ridge at eighteen, come back to haunt old familiar surroundings. This poised, sophisticated woman of twenty-two was as out of place in the battered pickup as Cade would be in a tuxedo at the Met.

"I guess you've all got your hands full," Abby remarked as they approached the sprawling ranch house.

"Damned straight," Hank said without preamble as he slowed at a gate. "Storm warnings out and calving in full swing."

"Snow?" she gasped, looking around at the lush greenery. But it was April, after all, and snow was still very possible in Montana. Worse—probable.

But Hank was already out of the truck, leaving the engine idling while he opened the gate.

"Drive the truck through!" he called for what seemed the tenth time in as many minutes, and Abby obediently climbed behind the wheel and put the truck in gear.

She couldn't help smiling when she remembered her childhood. Ranch children learned to drive early, out of necessity. She'd been driving a truck since her eleventh birthday, and many was the time she'd done it for Cade while he opened the endless gates that enclosed the thousands of acres he ranched.

She drove through the gate and slid back into her seat while Hank secured it and ambled back to the truck. He'd been part of Cade's outfit as long as she could remember, and there was no more experienced cowboy on the place.

"New York," Hank scoffed, giving her a disapproving glance. He chewed on the wad of tobacco in his cheek and gave a gruff snort. "Should have stayed home where you belonged. Been married by now, with a passel of younguns."

She shuddered at the thought, and her eyes clouded. "Is Cade at the ranch?" she asked, searching for something to say.

"Up in the Piper, hunting strays," he told her. "Figured he'd better find those damned cows before the snow hits. As it is, we'll have to fan out and bring them in to the barn. We lost over a hundred calves in the snow last spring."

Her pale eyes clouded at the thought of those tiny calves freezing to death. Cade had come home one winter night, carrying a little white-faced Hereford across his saddle, and Abby had helped him get it into the barn to warm it. He'd been tired and snappy and badly in need of a shave. Abby had fetched him a cup of coffee, and they'd stayed hours in the barn until the calf was thawed and on the mend. Even now, the memory made her grow warm. Cade was so much a part of her life, despite their quarrels. He was the only person she'd ever felt truly at home with.

"Are you listening?" Hank grumbled. "Honest to God, Abby!"

"Sorry, Hank," she apologized quickly as the elderly man glared at her. "What did you say?"

"I asked you if you wanted to stow your gear at the house or go on down to the homestead."

The "house" was Cade's—the main ranch house. The "homestead" had been her father's and was now Melly's. Soon, it would belong to Melly and her new husband.

"Where's Melly?"

"At the house."

"Then just drop me off there, please, Hank," she said with a pacifying smile.

He grunted and gunned the engine. A minute later, she was outside under the spreading branches of the budding trees and Hank was roaring away in a cloud of dust. Just like old times, she thought with a laugh. Hank impatient, dumping her at the nearest opportunity, while he rushed on to his chores.

Of course, it was nearing roundup, and that always made him irritable. It was late April now—by June, the ranch would be alive and teeming with activity as new calves were branded and separated and the men worked twenty-four-hour days and wondered why they had ever wanted to be cowboys.

She turned toward the house with a sigh. It was just as well that Cade wasn't home, she told herself. Seeing him now was going to be an ordeal. All she wanted was her sister.

She knocked at the door hesitantly, and seconds later, it was thrown open by a smaller girl with short golden hair and sea green eyes.

"Abby!" the younger girl burst out, tears appearing

in her eyes. She threw open the door and held out her arms.

Abby ran straight into them and held on for dear life, oblivious to the suitcase falling onto the cleanly swept front porch. She clutched her sister and cried like a lost child. She was home. She was safe.

2

"I was so glad when you decided to come." Melly sighed over coffee while she and Abby sat in the sprawling living room. It had changed quite a bit since Cade's mother died. The delicate antiques and pastel curtains had given way to leather-covered couches and chairs, handsome coffee tables and a luxurious, thick-piled grey rug. Now it looked like Cade—big and untamed and unchangeable.

"Sorry," Abby murmured when she realized she hadn't responded. "I had my mind on this room. It's changed."

Melly looked concerned. "A lot of things have. Cade included."

"Cade never changes," came the quiet reply. The taller girl got to her feet with her coffee cup in hand and wandered to the mantel, to stare at a portrait of Donavan McLaren that overwhelmed the room.

Cade was a younger version of the tall, imposing man in the painting, except that Donavan had white hair and a mustache and a permanent scowl. Cade's hair was still black and thick over a broad forehead and deep-set dark eyes. He was taller than his late father, all muscle. He was darkly tanned and he rarely smiled, but he could be funny in a dry sort of way. He was thirty-six now, fourteen years Abby's senior, although he seemed twice that judging by the way he treated her. Cade was always the patronizing adult to Abby's wayward child. Except for that one magic night when he'd been every woman's dream—when he'd shown her a taste of intimacy that had colored her life ever since, and had rejected her with such tenderness that she'd never been ashamed of offering herself to him.

Offering herself . . . she shuddered delicately, lifting the coffee to her lips. As if that would ever be possible again, now.

"How is Cade?" Abby asked.

"How is Cade usually in the spring?" came the amused reply.

"Oh, I can think of several adjectives. Would horrible be too mild?" Abby asked as she turned.

"Yes." Melly sighed. "We've been shorthanded. Randy broke his leg and won't be any use at all for five more weeks, and Hob quit."

"Hob?" Abby's pale brown eyes widened. "But he's been here forever!"

"He said that was just how he felt after Cade threw the saddle at him." The younger woman shook her head. "Cade's been restless. Even more so than usual."

"Woman trouble?" Abby asked, and then hated herself for the question. She had no right to pry into Cade's love life, no real desire to know if he were seeing someone.

Melly blinked. "Cade? My God, I'd faint if he brought a woman here."

That did come as a surprise. Although Abby had visited Melly several times since she'd moved to New York, she had seen Cade only on rare occasions. She'd always assumed that he was going out on dates while she was on Painted Ridge.

"I thought he kept them on computer, just so that he could keep track of them." Abby laughed.

"Are we talking about the same man?"

"Well, he's always out every time I come to visit," Abby remarked. "It's been almost a year since I've seen him." She sat back down on the sofa next to her sister and drained her coffee cup.

Melly shot her a keen glance, but she didn't reply. "How long are you going to stay?" she asked. "I never could pin you down on the phone."

"A couple of weeks, if you can put up with me. . . ."

"Don't be silly," Melly chided. She frowned, reaching out to touch her sister's thin hand. "Abby, make it a month. At least a month. Don't go back until you feel ready. Promise me!"

Abby's eyes closed under a tormented frown. She caught her breath. "I wonder if I'll ever be ready," she whispered roughly.

The smaller hand that was clasping hers tightened. "That's defeatist talk. And not like you at all. You're a Shane. We wrote the book on persevering!"

"Well, I'm writing the last chapter," Abby ground out. She stood up, moving to the window.

"It's been two weeks since it happened," Melly reminded her.

"Yes," Abby said, sighing wearily. "And I'm not quite as raw as I was, but it's hard trying to cope. . . ." She glanced at her sister. "I'm just glad I had the excuse of helping you plan the wedding to come for a visit. What did Cade say when you asked if it was all right?"

Melly looked thoughtful. "He brightened like a copper penny," she said with a faint smile. "Especially when I mentioned that you might be here for a couple of weeks or more. It struck me at the time, because he's been just the very devil to get along with lately."

Abby pursed her lips thoughtfully. "He probably has the idea that I've lost my job and came back in disgrace. Is that it?"

"Shame on you," her sister replied. "He'd never gloat over something like that."

"That's what you think. He's always hated the idea of my modeling."

Melly's thin brows rose. "Well, no matter what his opinion of your career, he was glad to hear you'd be around for a while. In fact, he was in such a good mood, all the men got nervous. Surely Hank told you that Hob had just quit? Too bad he didn't wait an extra day. Cade's bucking for sainthood since I announced your arrival."

If only it were true, Abby thought wistfully. But she knew better, even if Melly didn't. She was almost certain that Cade avoided her on purpose. Maybe it was just her sister's way of smoothing things over, to prevent a wild argument between Cade and Abby. It wouldn't be the first time she'd played peacemaker.

She glanced sharply into her sister's green eyes. "Melly, you didn't tell Cade the truth?" she asked anxiously.

Melly looked uncomfortable. "Not exactly," she confided. "I just said there was a man . . . that you'd had a bad experience."

Abby sighed. "Well, that's true enough. At least I'll be down at the homestead with you. He shouldn't even get suspicious about why I'm here. God knows, it's always been an uphill fight to keep peace when Cade and I are in the same room together, hasn't it?"

Melly shifted suddenly and Abby stared at her curiously.

"I'm afraid you won't be staying at the homestead," Melly said apologetically. "You see, my house is being painted. Cade's having the old place renovated as a wedding present."

Abby felt a wave of pure tension stretch her slender body. "We'll be staying . . . here?"

"Yes."

"Then why didn't you tell me when I asked to come?" Abby burst out.

"Because I knew you wouldn't come," Melly replied.

"Will Cade be away?" she asked.

"Are you kidding? In the spring, with roundup barely a month away?"

"Then I'll go somewhere else!" Abby burst out.

"No." Melly held her fast. "Abby, the longer you run away the harder it's going to be for you. Here, on the ranch, you can adjust again. You're going to have to adjust—or bury yourself. You do realize that? You can't possibly go on like this. Look at you!" she exclaimed, indicating the shapeless dress. "You don't even look like a model, Abby, you look like a housekeeper!"

"And that's a fine thing to say about me," came a deep but feminine voice from the doorway.

Both girls turned at once. Calla Livingston had her hands on her ample hips, and she was wearing a scowl sour enough to curdle milk. She was somewhere near sixty, but she could still outrun most of the cowboys, and few of them crossed her. She took her irritation out on the food, which was a shame because she was the best cook in the territory.

"And what do I look like, pray tell—the barn?" Calla continued, ruffled.

Melly bit her lip to keep from smiling. Dressed in a homemade shift of pink and green, her straggly grey hair pulled into a half-bun, her garter-supported hose hanging precariously just above her knees, Calla was nobody's idea of haute couture. But only an idiot would have told her that, and Melly had good sense.

"You look just fine, Calla," Melly soothed. "I meant"—she searched for the right words—"that this isn't Abby's usual look."

Calla burst out laughing, her merry eyes going from one girl to the other. "Never could tell when I was serious and when I wasn't, could you, darlin'?" she asked Melly. "I was only teasing. Come here, Abby, and give us a hug. It's been months since I've seen you, remember!"

Abby ran into her widespread arms and breathed in

the scent of flour and vanilla that always clung to Calla.

"Stay home this time, you hear?" Calla chided, brushing away a tear as she let go of the young woman. "Tearing off and coming back with city ways—this is the best you've looked to me since you were eighteen and hellbent on modeling!"

"But, Calla . . ." Melly interrupted.

"Never you mind." Calla threw her a sharp glance. "Call her dowdy again, and it'll be no berry cobbler for you tonight!"

Melly opened her mouth and quickly closed it again with a wicked grin. "I think she looks . . . mature," Melly agreed. "Very . . . unique. Unusual. Rustically charming."

Calla threw up her hands. "What I put up with, Lord knows! As if that hard-eyed cowboy I work for isn't enough on my plate. . . . Well, if I don't rush, there'll be no peace when he comes in and doesn't find his meal waiting. Even if he doesn't come in until ten o'clock." She went away muttering irritably to herself.

Melly sat down heavily on the couch with an exaggerated sigh. "Oh, saved! If I'd realized that she was out there, I'd have sung the praises of your new wardrobe."

"Still hooked on her berry cobbler, I notice?" Abby smiled, and for just an instant, a little of her old, vibrantly happy personality peeked out.

"Please tell him," Melly pleaded.

"And give him a stick to beat me with?" Abby asked with a dry laugh. "He's been down on me ever since I coaxed Dad into letting me go to New York. Every time I see him, all I hear is how stupid I was. Now he's got the best reason in the world to say it all again, and add an 'I told you so.' But he's not getting the chance, Melly. Not from me!"

"You're wrong about Cade," Melly argued. "You always have been. He doesn't hate you, Abby. He never did."

"Would you mind telling him that?" came the cool reply. "I don't think he knows."

"Then why was he so anxious for you to come home?" Melly demanded. She folded her arms across her knees and leaned forward. "He even had Hank bring up your own furniture from the homestead, just so you'd feel more at home. Does that sound like a man who's hating you?"

"Then why does he avoid me like the plague?" Abby asked curtly. She searched momentarily for a way to change the subject. "I sure would like to freshen up before we eat," she hinted.

"Then come on up. You've got the room next to mine, so we can talk until all hours."

"I'll like that," Abby murmured with a smile. Impulsively, she put her arm around Melly's shoulders as they went up the staircase. "Maybe we can have a pillow fight, for old time's sake."

"Calla's room is across the hall," Melly informed her.

Abby sighed. "Oh, well, we can always reminisce about the pillow fights we used to have," she amended, and Melly grinned.

It was just after dark, and Melly was helping Calla set the table in the dining room when the front door slammed open and hard, angry footsteps sounded on the bare wood floor of the hall.

Abby, standing at the fireplace where Calla had built a small fire, turned just as Cade froze in the doorway.

It didn't seem like a year since she'd seen him. The hard, deeply tanned face under that wide-brimmed hat was as familiar as her own. But he'd aged, even she could see that. His firm, chiseled mouth was compressed, his brow marked with deep lines as if he'd made a habit of scowling. His cheeks were leaner, his square jaw firmer and his dark, fiery eyes were as uncompromising as she remembered them.

He was dusted with snow, his shepherd's coat flecked with it, his worn boots wet with it as were the batwing chaps strapped around his broad, heavy-muscled thighs. He was holding a cigarette in one lean, dark hand, and the look he was giving Abby would have backed down a puma.

"What the hell happened to you?" he asked curtly, indicating the shapeless brown suede dress she was wearing.

"Look who's talking," she returned. "Weren't you wearing that same pair of chaps when I left for New York?"

"Cattlemen are going bust all over, honey," he returned, and a hint of amusement kindled in his eyes.

"Sure," she scoffed. "But most of them don't run eight thousand head of cattle on three ranches in two states, now do they? And have oil leases and mining contracts. . . ."

"I didn't say I was going bust," he corrected. He leaned insolently against the doorjamb and tilted his head back. "Steal that dress off a fat lady?"

She felt uncomfortable, shifting from one foot to the other. "It's the latest style," she lied, hoping he wouldn't know the difference.

"I don't see how you women keep up with the latest styles," he said. "It all looks like odds and ends to me."

"Is it snowing already?" she asked, changing the subject.

He took his hat off and shook it. "Looks like. I hope Calla's loading a table for the men, too. The nighthawks are going to have their hands full with those two-year-old heifers."

Abby couldn't help smiling. Those were the first-time mothers, and they took a lot of looking after. One old cowhand—Hob, the one who'd resigned—always said he'd rather mend fence than babysit new mamas.

"Who got stuck this year?" she asked.

"Hank and Jeb," he replied.

"No wonder Hank was so ruffled," she murmured.

A corner of Cade's disciplined mouth turned up as he studied her. "You don't know the half of it. He begged me to let him nurse the older cows."

"I can guess how far he got," she said.

He didn't laugh. "How long are you here for?"

"I haven't decided yet," she said, feeling nervous. "It depends."

"I thought spring was your busiest time, miss model," he said, his eyes narrowing suspiciously. "When Melly told me you were coming, it surprised me."

"I'm, uh, taking a break," she supplied.

"Are you?" He shouldered away from the doorjamb. "Stay through roundup and I'll fly you back to New York myself."

He turned, and her eyes followed his broad-shouldered form as he walked into the hall and yelled for Calla.

"I hope you've got enough to feed the hands, too!" he called, his deep voice carrying through the house. "Jeb's nighthawking with Hank!"

Jeb was the bunkhouse cook—some of the cowboys had homes on the ranch where they lived with their families, but there was a modern bunkhouse with a separate kitchen for the rest.

"Well, I'll bet the boys are on their knees giving thanks for that!" Calla called back. "It'll be a change for them, having decent food for one night!"

Cade chuckled deep in his throat as he climbed the stairs. Abby couldn't help but watch him, remembering old times when she'd worshipped that broad back, that powerful body, with a schoolgirl's innocent heart. How different her life might have been if Cade hadn't refused her impulsive offer that long-ago night. Tears formed in her eyes and she turned away. Wishing wouldn't make it so. But it was good to be back on Painted Ridge, all the same. She'd manage to keep out of Cade's way, and perhaps Melly was right. Perhaps being home again would help her scars to heal.

3

Abby might have planned to avoid him, but Cade seemed to have other ideas. She noticed his quiet, steady gaze over the dinner table and almost jumped when he spoke.

"How would you like to see the new calves?" he asked suddenly.

She lifted her eyes from her plate and stared at him, lost for an answer. "Isn't it still snowing?" she asked helplessly.

"Sure," he agreed. "But the trucks have chains. And the calving sheds are just south of here," he reminded her.

Being alone with him was going to unnerve her—she knew it already—but she loved the sight of those woolly little creatures, so new to the world. And she liked being with Cade. She felt safe with him, protected. Despite the lingering apprehension, she wanted to go with him.

"Well?" he persisted.

She shrugged. "I would kind of like to see the calves," she admitted with a tiny smile. She dropped her eyes back to her plate, blissfully unaware of the look Cade exchanged with Melly.

"We'll have dessert when we get back," Cade informed Calla, pushing back his chair.

Minutes later, riding along in the pickup and being bounced wildly in its warm interior, snow fluttering against the windshield, it was almost like old times.

"Warm enough, honey?" Cade asked.

"Like toast." She wrapped the leather jacket he had loaned her even closer, loving its warmth. Cade was still wearing his shepherd's coat, looking so masculine he'd have wowed them even at a convention of male models.

"Not much further now," he murmured, turning the truck off onto the farm road that led to the calving pens, where two cowboys in yellow slickers could be seen riding around the enclosures, heads bent against the wind.

"Poor devils," she remarked, watching.

"The men or the heifers?" he asked.

"Both. All. It's rough out there." She balanced her hand against the cold dashboard as he stopped the truck and cut the engine at the side of the long shed. Cade was the perfect rancher, but his driving left a lot to be desired.

"Now I know how it feels to ride inside a concrete mixer," she moaned.

"Don't start that again," Cade grumbled as he threw open the door. "You can always walk back," he added with a dark glance.

"Did you ever race in the Grand Prix when you were younger, Cade?" she asked with a bright, if somewhat false, smile.

"And sarcasm won't do the trick, either," he warned. He led the way through the snow, and she followed in his huge footprints, liking the bite of the cold wind and the crunch of the snow, the freshness of the air. It was so deliciously different from the city. Her eyes looked out over the acres toward the distant mountains, searching for the familiar snow-covered peaks that she could have seen clearly in sunny daylight. God's country, she thought reverently. How had she ever been able to exist away from it?

"Stop daydreaming and catch up," Cade was growling. "I could lose you out here."

"In a little old spring snowstorm like this?" She laughed. "I could fight my way through blizzards, snowshoe myself to Canada, ski over to the Rockies . . ."

". . . lie like hell, too," he said, amusement gleaming in the dark eyes that caught hers as they entered the lighted interior. "Come on."

She followed him into the airy enclosure, wrapping her arms tight. "Still no heat, I see." She sighed.

"Can't afford the luxury, honey," he remarked, waving at a cowboy further down the aisle.

"Is that why it's so drafty in here? You poor thing, you," she chided.

"I would be, if I didn't keep the air circulating in here," he agreed. "Don't you remember how many calves we used to lose to respiratory ailments before the veterinarians advised us to put in that exhaust fan to keep stale air out of these sheds? Those airborne diseases were bankrupting the operation. Now we disinfect the stalls and maintain a rigid vaccination program, and we've cut our losses in half."

"Excuse me," she apologized. "I'm only an ignorant city dweller."

He turned in the aisle and looked down at her quietly. "Come home," he said curtly. "Where you belong."

Her heart pounded at the intensity of the brief gaze he gave her before turning back to his cow boss.

Charlie Smith stood up, grinning at Cade. "Hi, boss, get tired of television and hungry for some real relaxation? Jed sure would love to have somebody take his place—"

"Just visiting, Charlie," Cade interrupted. "I brought Abby down to see the newcomers."

"Good to see you again, Miss Abby," Charlie said respectfully, tipping his hat. "We've got a good crop in here, all right. Have a look."

Abby peeked into the nearest stall, her face lighting up as she stared down at one of the "black baldies," a cross between a Hereford and a Black Angus, black all over with a little white face.

"Jed brought that one in an hour ago. Damn . . . uh, doggone mama just dropped it and walked away from it." Charlie sneered.

"That's not his mama, huh?" Abby murmured, noticing the tender licking it was getting from the cow in the stall with it.

"No, ma'am," Charlie agreed. "We sprayed him with a deodorizing compound to keep her from getting suspicious. Poor thing lost her own calf."

Abby felt a surge of pity for the cow and calf. It was

just a normal episode in ranch life, but she had a hard time trying to separate business from emotion.

Cade moved close behind her, apparently oblivious to the sudden, instinctive stiffening of her slender body, the catch of her breath. Please, she thought silently, please don't let him touch me!

But he didn't attempt to. He leaned against the stall and rammed his hands in his pockets, watching the cow and calf over her shoulder. "How many have we lost so far?" Cade asked the cow boss.

"Ten. And it looks like a long night."

"They're all long." Cade sighed. He pushed his hat back over his forehead, and Abby, glancing up, noticed how weary he looked.

"I'd better check on my own charge down the aisle here," Charlie said, and went off with a wave of his hand as the ominous bleating of the heifer filled the shed.

"Prime beef," Cade murmured, chuckling at Abby's indignant expression.

She moved away from him with studied carelessness and smiled. "Heartless wretch," she teased. "Could you really eat him?"

"Couldn't you, smothered in onions . . . ?"

"Oh, stop!" she wailed. "You cannibal . . . !"

"How does it feel to be back?" he asked, walking back the way they came in.

"Nice," she admitted. She tucked her cold hands into the pockets of her jacket. "I'd forgotten how big this country is, how unspoiled and underpopulated. It's a wonderful change from a crowded, polluted city, although I do love New York," she added, trying to convince him she meant it.

"New York," he reminded her, "is a dangerous place."

She stiffened again, turning to study his face, but she couldn't read anything in that bland expression. Cade let nothing show—unless he wanted it to. He'd had years of practice at camouflaging his emotions.

"Most cities are," she agreed. "The country can be dangerous, too."

"It depends on your definition of danger," he returned. He looked down at her with glittering eyes. "You're safe as long as I'm alive. Nothing and no one will hurt you on this ranch."

Tears suddenly misted her eyes, burning like fire. She swallowed and looked away. "Do I look as if I need protection?" She tried to laugh.

"Not especially," he said coolly. "But you seemed threatened for an instant. I just wanted to make the point. I'll protect you from mountain lions and falling buildings, Abby," he added with a hint of a smile.

"But who'll protect me from you, you cannibal?" she asked with a pointed stare, her old sense of humor returning to save her from the embarrassment of tears.

"You're just as safe with me as you want to be," he replied.

She looked into his eyes, and for an instant they were four years in the past, when a young girl stood poised at the edge of a swimming pool and offered her heart and her body to a man she worshipped.

Without another word, she turned around and started back out into the snow.

4

As she walked toward the truck, huddled against the wind, her mind suddenly went backward in time. And for an instant, it was summer, and she was swimming alone in the pool at Cade's house one night when her father was in the hospital.

She'd been eighteen, a girl on the verge of becoming a woman. Her father, far too ill during that period of her life to give her much counsel, hadn't noticed that she was beginning to dress in a way that caught a lot of male attention. But Cade had, and he'd had a talk with her. She'd marched off in a huff, hating his big-brother attitude, and had defiantly gone for a swim that night in his own pool. There was no one around, so she had quickly stripped off her clothes and dived in. That was against the rules, but Abby was good at breaking them. Especially when they were made by Cade McLaren. She wanted him to look at her the way other men did. She wanted more than a condescending lecture from him, but she was too young and far too naive to put her growing infatuation into words.

She'd been in the pool barely five minutes when she heard the truck pull up at the back of the house. Before she had time to do any more than scramble out of the pool and pull on her jeans, she heard Cade come around the corner.

She was totally unprepared for what happened next. She turned and Cade's dark eyes dropped to her high, bare breasts with a wild, reckless look in them that made her breath catch in her throat. He just stood there, frozen, staring at her, and she didn't make a move to cover herself or turn away. She let him look his fill, feeling her heart trying to tear out of her chest when he finally began to move toward her.

His shirt was open that night, because he'd just come in from the corral, and the mat of thick black hair over the bronzed muscles of his chest was damp with sweat. He stopped a foot in front of her and looked down, and she knew that all the unspoken hunger she'd begun to feel for him was plain in her wide, pale brown eyes.

Without a word, he bent and lifted her. Very, very gently, he brought her body to his and drew her taut breasts against his chest, letting her feel the rough hair against her soft, sensitive skin in a caress that made her moan and cling to him, while her eyes looked straight into his and saw the flash of triumph in them.

He turned and carried her into the house, up the stairs and into his own bedroom, and laid her down on the bed. And then he sat there, with one hand on the bed beside her to support his weight, and looked at her again, letting his dark eyes feast on the soft, pink bareness of her body. She wasn't even aware of being wet, of her body soaking the coverlet. All she saw, all she knew, was Cade's hard, dark face and his eyes.

Finally, he moved and his fingers traced a pattern from her shoulder down over her collarbone. She held her breath as they kept going down, and she felt the slow, sweet tracing of them on the curve of her breasts—exploring, tantalizing with the light pressure—until they reached the burgeoning peak and caught it lightly between them.

She gasped, arching at the unexpected surge of pleasure, and his eyes looked straight down into hers.

"Hush," he whispered then. "You know I won't hurt you."

"Yes," she whispered back, as if the walls could hear them, her eyes wide with unexpected pleasure. "I . . . I want you . . . to touch me."

"I know." He bent, one hand still cupping her, and she lifted her arms hesitantly until they were around his neck. He looked into her eyes as his warm, hard mouth brushed hers, so that he could see the reaction in them. "Open your mouth for me, Abby," he breathed, moving his hand to tip up her chin, "just a little more. . . ."

She obeyed him mindlessly and felt the delicious probing of his tongue between her lips, working its way slowly, sensuously, into her mouth. She gasped, moaning, and he eased down so that she could feel his bare chest against her breasts. She lifted herself, clinging, and for one long, unbearably sweet moment she felt his warmth and weight and the fierce adult passion of a man's kiss.

She thought she imagined a tremor in his hard arms before he suddenly released her, but when he sat up again he was as calm outwardly as if he'd been for a quiet walk. His eyes went down to her breasts and drank in the sight of them one last time before his big hand caught the coverlet and tossed it carelessly over her bareness.

"You wanted to know," he said gently, holding her hand tightly in his as if to soften the rejection. "And I've shown you. But this is as far as it goes. I care too much to seduce you just for an hour of pleasure."

She swallowed, studying his hard face, her body still tingling from the touch of his fingers, her mouth warm from the long, hungry kiss they'd shared. "Should I be ashamed, Cade?" she asked.

He brushed the damp hair away from her face. "Of what?" he asked tenderly. "Of wanting to know how it felt to be touched and kissed by a man?"

She drew in a deep, slow breath. "Not . . . by a man," she corrected. "By you."

The impact of that nervous confession was evident on his face. He hesitated, as if he wanted desperately to say something but thought better of it. His jaw tautened.

"Abby," he said, choosing the words carefully, "you're eighteen years old. You've got a lot of growing up to do, a lot of the world to see, before you tie yourself to one man. To any man." He toyed with the coverlet at her throat. "It's natural, at your age, to be curious about sex. But despite the modern viewpoint, there are still men left who'll want a virgin when they marry." His eyes met hers levelly. "Be one. Save that precious gift for the man you marry. Don't give it away to satisfy your curiosity."

"Will you?" she asked involuntarily.

"Will I what, honey?" he asked.

"Want a virgin?"

He looked strange at that moment. Thoughtful. Hungry. Irritated. "The biggest problem in my life," he said after a minute, with a flash of humor, "is that I want one right now." He bent then and kissed her briefly, roughly, before he stood up.

"Cade . . . ?" she began, her hand going to the coverlet, the offer in her young eyes.

"No," he said firmly, loosening her fingers from the material. "Not yet."

"Yet?" she whispered.

He traced her mouth with a lazy, absent finger. "Make me the same offer again in about three or four years," he murmured with a faint smile, "and I'll drag you into a bed and make love to you until you pass out. Now get dressed. And don't try this again, Abby," he warned firmly. "It's the wrong time for us. Don't force me to be cruel to you. It's something I'd have hell living with."

Her head whirling with unbridled hope, she watched him walk to the door with her whole heart in her misty eyes.

"Cade?" she called softly.

He'd turned with one hand on the doorknob, an eyebrow raised.

"I'll hold you to that . . . in three or four years," she promised.

He smiled back at her, so tenderly that she almost

climbed out of the bed and threw herself at his feet. "Goodnight, honey," he chuckled, walking out the door.

Neither of them had ever mentioned it, or referred to it, in all the time since then. Shortly afterward she had left the ranch; she'd seen Cade only a few times in the intervening years. It was odd that she should remember the incident now, when her promise was impossible to keep. She'd never be able to offer herself to Cade now.

She opened the door of the truck and got in.

Cade was quiet on the way back to the house, but that wasn't unusual. He never had liked to talk and drive at the same time. He seemed to mull over problems in the silence, ranch problems that were never far away. In winter, it was snow and getting enough feed to the livestock. In spring it was roundup and planting. In summer it was haying and fixing fence and water. Water was an eternal problem—there was either not enough or too much. In May and June, when the snow melted on the mountains and ran into streams and rivers, there would be enough water for agriculture—but there would also be flooding to contend with. After roundup, the cattle had to be moved to high summer pastures. In fall, they had to be brought back down. The breeding program was an ongoing project, and there were always the problems of sick cattle and equipment breakdowns and the logistics of feeding, culling, selling and buying cattle. Cade had ranch managers, like Melly's husband-to-be, but he owned three ranches, and ultimately he was the one responsible to the board of directors and to the stockholders as well. Because it was a corporation now, not just one man's holdings, and Cade was at the helm.

Her eyes sought his face, loving it as she'd loved it for four, long, empty years. Cade, the eternal bachelor. She wondered if he'd ever marry, or want children of his own to inherit Painted Ridge and the other properties he had stock in. She'd thought once, at eighteen, that he might marry her one day. But he'd made a point of avoiding her after that devastating encounter. And in desperation, she had settled for the adventure and challenge of modeling.

It had been the ultimate adventure at eighteen. Glamour, wealth, society—and for the first year or so it had almost satisfied her. She remembered coming home that first Christmas, bubbling with enthusiasm for her work. Cade had listened politely and then had left. And he'd been conspicuously absent for the rest of the time she was at Painted Ridge. She'd often wondered why he deliberately avoided her. But she'd been ecstatic over the glitter of New York and her increasing successes. Or she had been at first . . .

Cade seemed to sense her intense appraisal. His head suddenly turned and he caught her eyes as he pulled up to the house and parked at the back steps. Abby felt a shock of pure sensation go through her like fire. It had been a long time since she'd looked into those dark, glittering eyes at point-blank range. It did the most wonderful things to her pulse, her senses.

"You've been away longer this time," he said without preamble. He leaned back against his door and lit a cigarette. "A year."

"Not from the ranch," she countered. "You weren't here last summer or at Christmas when I was."

He laughed shortly, the cigarette sending up curls of smoke. "What was the use?" he asked coolly. "I got sick of hearing about New York and all the beautiful people."

She sat erect, her chin thrusting forward. "Are we going to have that argument all over again?"

"No, I'm through arguing," he said curtly. "You made up your mind four years ago that you couldn't find what you wanted from life anyplace except New York. I left you to it, Abby. I know a lost cause when I see one."

"What was there for me here?" she demanded, thinking back to a time when he wouldn't come near her.

But his face went cold at the words. It seemed actually to pale, and he turned his eyes out the window to look at the falling snow. "Nothing, I guess," he said. "Open country, clean air, basic values and only few people. Amazing, isn't it, that we have the fourth largest state in the country, but it's forty-sixth in population. And I like it that way," he added, pinning her with his eyes. "I couldn't live in a place where I didn't have enough room to walk without being bumped into."

She knew that already. Cade, with his long, elegant stride and love of open country, might as well die as be transplanted to New York. This was Big Sky country, and he was a Big Sky man. He'd never feel at home in the Big Apple. A hundred years ago, however, he would have fit right in with the old frontier ways. She remembered going to the old Custer battlefield with him, where the Battle of the Little Bighorn was fought, and watching his eyes sweep the rolling hills. He sat a horse the same way, his eyes always on the horizon. One of his ancestors had been a full-blooded Sioux, and had died at Little Bighorn. He belonged to this country, as surely as the early settlers and miners and cattlemen had belonged to it.

Abby had wanted to belong to it, too—to Cade. But he'd let her get on that bus to New York when she was eighteen, although he'd had one hell of a fight with her father about it the night before she left. Jesse Shane had never shared the discussion with her. She only knew about it because she'd heard their angry voices in the living room and her name on Cade's lips.

"You never wanted me to go to New York," she murmured as she withdrew from the pain of memory. "You expected me to fall flat on my face, didn't you?"

"I hoped like hell that you would," he said bluntly, and his eyes blazed. "But you made it, didn't you? Although, looking at you now, I could almost believe you hadn't. My God, Calla has better taste in clothes."

She avoided his eyes, puzzled by the earlier statement. "I'm very tastefully dressed for a woman on a ranch," she threw back, nervous that he might guess why she was wearing loose clothing, why she couldn't bear anything revealing right now.

"Is that a dig at me?" he asked. "I know ranch life isn't glamorous, honey. It's damned hard work, and not many women would choose it over a glittering career. You don't have to tell me that."

How little he knew, she thought miserably. She'd chuck modeling and New York and the thought of being internationally famous if he asked her to marry him. She would have given up anything to live with him and love him. But he didn't know, and he never would. Her pride wouldn't let her tell him. He'd rejected her once, that magic night years before, even though he did it tenderly. She couldn't risk having him do it again. It would be too devastating.

Her eyes dropped to her suede boots. The boots would be ruined. She'd forgotten to spray them with protective coating, and she'd need to buy a new pair. Odd that she should think about that when she was alone with Cade. It was so precious to be alone with him, even for a few minutes. If only she could tell him what had happened, tell him the truth. But how could she admit that she'd come back to be healed?

"Hey."

She looked up and found him watching her closely. He reached out and caught a lock of her long hair and tugged it gently.

"What's wrong?" he asked quietly.

She felt the prick of tears and blinked to dispel them. It was so much harder when he was tender. It reminded her forcibly of the last time she'd heard his voice so velvety and deep. And suddenly she found herself wondering how she would react if he tried to hold her, touch her, now.

"Nothing's wrong," she said shortly. "I was just thinking."

His face hardened and he let go of her hair. "Thinking about New York?" he demanded. "What the hell are you doing here in April, anyway? I thought summer was your only slack time."

"I came to see Melly, of course," she shot back, her face hot and red. "To help her get ready for the wedding!"

"Then you'll be staying for a month," he said matter-of-factly, daring her to protest. How could she when she'd stated the lie so convincingly?

She swallowed. "Well . . ."

"I understood you were designing her a dress?" he continued.

"Yes," she agreed, remembering the sketches she'd already done. Over the last few years she had discovered that she enjoyed designing clothes much more than modeling them.

"My God, you're quiet," he observed, his eyes narrowing against the smoke of his cigarette. "You used to come home gushing like a volcano, full of life and happiness. Now you seem . . . sedate. Very, very different. What's the matter, honey, is the glitter wearing off, or are you just tired of going around half-naked for men to look at?"

She gasped at the unexpectedness of the attack and drew in a sharp breath. "Cade Alexander McLaren, I do not go around half-naked!"

"Don't you?" he demanded. He had that old familiar look on his face, the one that meant he was set for a fight. "I was up in New York one day last month on business and I went to one of your fashion shows. You were wearing a see-through blouse with nothing under it. Nothing!" His face hardened. "My God, I almost went up there and dragged you off that runway. It was all I could do to turn around and walk out of the building. Your father would have rolled over in his grave!"

"My father was proud of me," she returned, hurting from the remark. "And unless you missed it, most of the people who go to those shows are women!"

"There were men there," he came back. He crushed out the cigarette. "Do you take off your clothes for men in private, too, Abby?"

She lifted her hand to hit him, but he caught the wrist and jerked. She found herself looking straight into his narrowed eyes at an alarming distance. But worse, she felt the full force of his strength in that steely grip, and she felt panic rise in her throat.

"Let me go, Cade," she said suddenly, her voice ghostly, her eyes widening with fear. "Oh, please, let me go!"

He scowled, freeing her all at once. She drew back against her door like a cornered cat, actually trembling with reaction. Well, now she knew, didn't she? she thought miserably. She'd wondered how she'd react to Cade's strength, and now she truly knew.

"Remember me?" he asked angrily. "We've known each other most of our lives. I was defending myself, Abby. I wasn't going to hit you. What the hell's the matter with you? Has some man been knocking you around?" His face became frankly dangerous. "Answer me," he said harshly. "Has one of your boyfriends been rough with you? By God, if he has . . . !"

"No, it's not that," she said quickly, drawing in a steadying breath. Her eyes closed on a wave of remorse. "I'm just tired, Cade. Tired. Burned out. Too many long hours and too many go-sees that didn't work out, too many demanding photographers, too many retakes of commercials, too many fittings, too many temperamental designers. . . ." She slumped back against the door and opened her eyes, weary eyes, to look at him. "I'm tired." It was a lie, but then, how could she possibly tell him the truth?

"You came home to rest, is that what you're telling me?" he asked softly.

"Is it all right?" she asked, her eyes searching his. "A whole month, and I don't want to interfere with your life. . . ."

"That's a joke," he scoffed. His eyes went over the shapeless dress. "You don't know what a joke it is." He turned abruptly to open the door. "Let's go in. It's freezing out here. We can sit around inside for the rest of the night and watch your sister and Jerry climb all over each other."

He sounded utterly disgusted, and she laughed involuntarily. "They're engaged," she reminded him.

"Then why don't they get married and make out in their own house?" he growled.

"They're trying," she said.

He gave her a hard glare before he opened his door and went around to open hers. "The wedding can't be soon enough to suit me," he said. "The only place I haven't caught them at it is in a closet."

"They're in love." She stepped down from the running board, landing in the soft, cold snow. "My gosh, you're old-fashioned, Cade."

"Don't tell me you hadn't noticed that before?" he asked as they walked toward the house through the driving snow. It tickled Abby's face, melting cold and wet over her delicate features.

"It's hard to miss," she agreed. She glanced up at him, walking so tall and straight beside her. He moved with easy grace, long strides that marked him an outdoorsman. It would take wide-open country like Montana to hold him. "But people in love are notoriously hard to separate."

"What would you know about love?" he asked, shooting a glance down at her. "Have you ever felt it?"

She laughed with brittle humor. "Most people have a crush or two in a lifetime."

"You had one on me once, as I remember," he said quietly. He was staring straight ahead, or he'd have seen the shock that widened Abby's pale brown eyes.

"I'm surprised you even noticed," she muttered. "In between raising cattle and fighting off girls at square dances."

"I noticed." The words didn't mean a lot, but the way he said them did. There was a world of meaning in the curt, harsh sound of them.

She drew in a slow breath and wrapped her arms around her chest, averting her gaze from him. Would she ever forget that night? Despite the recent experience that had soured physical relationships for her, she felt an explosion of pleasure at the memory of Cade's warm, rough mouth on her own, his hands touching her so gently. . . .

They were at the back door. He opened it and let her into the warm, dry kitchen ahead of him. Calla had apparently stepped out for a minute, because it was deserted.

"Abby," he called.

She turned at the entrance to the dining room and looked back at him. He'd pulled off his hat, and his dark hair glittered damply black in the light.

His eyes slid down her body, taking in the ill-fitting

clothing, and went back up to her flushed face and wide, soft eyes. The tension was suddenly between them, the old tension that she'd felt that night at the swimming pool when he'd seen her as no other man ever had. She could feel the shock of his gaze, the wild beat of her own heart in the silence that throbbed with unexpected promise.

"Are you happy in New York?" he asked.

She faltered, trying to get words past her tight throat. She had been—or she'd convinced herself that she had been—until the incident that had made her run home for shelter, for comfort. But always she'd missed Painted Ridge . . . and Cade.

"Of course I am," she lied. "Why?"

His tall frame shifted impatiently, as if he'd wanted an answer she hadn't given him. He made a strange gesture with one hand. "I just wondered, that's all. I saw your face on a magazine cover the other day," he added, studying her. "One of the better ones. That means something, I gather?"

"Yes," she agreed with a wan smile. "It's quite a coup to have a cover on that kind of magazine. My agency was thrilled about it."

His eyes wandered over her face, searching eyes that grew dark with some emotion she couldn't name. "You're beautiful, all right," he said quietly. "You always were. Not just physically, either. You reminded me of sunlight on a morning meadow. All silky and bright and sweet to look at. Whatever happened to that little girl?"

She felt an ache deep inside, a hunger that nothing had ever filled. Her eyes touched every hard line of his face, lines she would have loved to smooth away. She withered away from you, she wanted to tell him. Part of her died when she left Painted Ridge.

But of course she couldn't say that. "She grew up, Cade," she said instead.

He shook his head and smiled—a strange, soft smile that puzzled her. "No, not quite. I carry her around in my memory and every once in a while, I take her out and look at her."

"She was dreadfully naive," she murmured, trying not to let him see how his statement had touched her.

He moved slowly toward her, stopping just in front of her. He towered over her, powerful and big and faintly threatening, and she fought down the fear of his strength that had already surfaced once that night.

She looked up, intrigued by the smell of leather and wind that clung to him. "I'd forgotten how tall you are," she said involuntarily.

"I've forgotten nothing about you, Abby," he said curtly. "Including the fact that once you couldn't get close enough to me. But now you back away the minute I come near you."

So he had noticed. She dropped her eyes to the front of his shepherd's coat. "Do I?"

"You shied away from me in the calving shed tonight. Do you think I didn't notice? Then in the truck . . ." He drew in a deep breath. "My God, I'd never hurt you. Don't you know that?"

Her eyes traced the stitching on the coat and she noticed a tiny smudge near one of the buttons, as if ashes from his cigarette had fallen on it. Silly things to be aware of when she could feel the heat of his big body, and she remembered as if it were yesterday how sweet it was to be held against him.

"I know," she said after a minute. She forced her eyes up to his. "I . . . have some problems I'm trying to work out."

"A man?" he asked curtly.

She nodded. "In a way."

His face hardened, and his hands came up as if he would have liked to grip her with them. But he abruptly jammed them into his pockets. "Want to tell me about it?"

Her head went slowly from side to side. "Not yet. I have to find myself, Cade. I have to work it out in my own way."

"Does it have something to do with your career?" he asked.

"Yes, it does. I have to decide whether or not I want to go on with it," she confessed.

He seemed to brighten. His face changed, relaxed, making him look strangely young. "Thinking of quitting?"

"Why not?" she asked, grinning. "Need an extra cowhand? I close gates good; you ask Hank if I don't."

He smiled back, his dark eyes sparkling with humor. "I'll do that."

She sighed. "You'll be ready to run me off by the time that month's up," she said with a short laugh. "Anyway, I've got a lot of thinking to do."

He searched her quiet face. "Maybe I can help you make up your mind," he murmured. One hand caught her chin and turned it up, while his eyes searched hers curiously. "Melly said there was a man. A bad experience. What happened, honey, a love affair gone sour?"

She flinched, moving backward to release herself

from the disturbing pressure of his fingers. She hadn't fled New York only to wind up back in Cade McLaren's hip pocket again; letting him get too close would be suicide in more ways than one. His strength unnerved her, but there was more to it than that. She reacted to him in ways that she'd never reacted to any other man. Every man she'd dated or been with socially had been for her a poor imitation of this one, and she was only now realizing how large he loomed in her memory. For years she'd pushed that night at the swimming pool to the back of her mind, afraid to take it out and look at it. And tonight, going back in time had stirred something deep inside her, had momentarily banished the bad memories to make way for remembered sensations and longings.

She stared up into Cade's dark eyes and saw her whole world. He was as big as this country, and nothing she ever found in New York was going to replace him. But there was no way she was going to let him know it. He'd pushed her away ever since that long-ago night. It was as if he couldn't bear having her close to him, in any way. Even now, when she backed away, he wasn't following. He could still let her go without flinching, without regret, even in this small way.

"A man," she agreed, and let it go at that, not looking at him. "What do you think I did in New York, stare out windows longing to be back here?" That was the truth, little did he know it. The glitter had long ago worn off her life, leaving it barren and lonely.

"Not me, honey," he said. "I know all too well how dull this place is to you. You've done everything but shout it from the roof." He glared at her. "Did the man come too close, Abby? Did he want to settle down, and you couldn't face the thought of that?"

She stared at him blankly. "Is that shocking?" she asked, adding fuel to the fire. "I told you, Cade, I like my life the way it is. I like having money to spend and things to see and places to go. I went to Jamaica to do a layout last month, and in September I'm going to Greece for another one. That's exciting; it's great fun."

He stared at her with cold eyes, believing the lie. "Yes, I can see that," he growled.

He pulled a cigarette from his pocket and lit it while his eyes ran quietly over every line of her face. "Then where does your boyfriend come in?"

She swallowed and turned away. "He wasn't . . . a boyfriend, and it's a long story."

"I'll find time to listen."

She shifted restlessly and turned. "Not tonight, if you don't mind. I'd like to say hello to Jerry."

He drew in an angry breath, and for just an instant she thought he was going to insist. But he reached past her and opened the door.

She went ahead of him, relieved that he'd swallowed her explanation. Boyfriend! Oh, God, what a horrible joke that was, but she'd rather have died than tell him the truth. Anyway, what would it matter? Let him think she was just getting over a love affair. What did it matter?

5

Melly was curled up on the sofa next to the tall, blond man who was going to be her husband. They both jumped when Cade deliberately slammed the door behind Abby and himself.

"Oh, hi, boss." Jerry Ridgely grinned, looking over the sofa back with dancing blue eyes. "Hi, Abby, welcome home!"

"Thanks, Jerry," she said, grinning back. She'd known him almost as long as Melly had. One of the advantages of growing up in country like this was that you knew most everybody from childhood onward. It gave people a sense of security to know that some things stayed constant.

"Staying for the wedding?" he asked, and Melly smiled at her sister.

"I wouldn't miss it for the world," she promised. "Which reminds me, Melly," she added, sticking her hands in her pockets, "I've roughed out some sketches for your wedding dress. They're in my suitcase."

"I'd love to see them," Melly said, enthusiastic. "You're sure you don't mind making it for me?"

"Don't be silly, of course I don't mind. Sometimes I wonder why I got into modeling when I love designing so much." Abby sighed. Modeling. The word reminded her of New York, which brought back other memories, and she turned away, her eyes clouding.

Melly got to her feet quickly. "Let's go see if Calla has the berry cobbler dished out," she said, catching Abby's arm. "Can you men live without us?"

"Cade can." Jerry laughed, glancing toward the taciturn rancher. "But I'll have trouble, sweetheart, so hurry, will you?"

"Sure," Melly agreed, in a tone that was meant for the foreman alone. She winked and tugged Abby along with her, closing the door behind them.

"Have you and Cade been at it again?" she asked Abby as soon as the door was closed behind them. "He looks like a thundercloud, and you're flushed."

"He's persistent as all get-out," Abby groaned. "He nearly backed me into a corner in the kitchen just now. He's not going to worm it out of me, Melly. I can't talk to him about it, I can't!"

Melly sighed and hugged her sister. "Oh, Abby, I hoped you might be able to, once the two of you were alone."

"Talk to Cade?" She laughed. "My God, all I have time to do is defend myself. He's even worse than I remembered. Why does he hate my career so much?"

"You really don't know, do you?" Melly murmured.

Abby ignored that, wrapping her arms tight around herself. "We got into it in the truck, and I tried to hit him, and when he grabbed my wrist . . ." She shivered. "He's so strong. . . ."

"He's also Cade," she was reminded. "He'd never hurt you, not the longest day he lived."

Abby tried to smile. "I want a miracle, I guess. I want Cade to touch me and make the fear all go away."

"That could still happen," Melly said softly. "But you have to give it time. And telling Cade the truth would be a heck of a start. For God's sake, Abby, it wasn't your fault . . . !"

"So everyone tells me." She sighed. "Let's go help Calla. I just want to get my mind on something else right now. It will all work out somehow, I suppose. Someday."

She carried that thought all through the long evening, watching Cade sit in his big chair and smoke cigarette after cigarette while he went over paperwork with Jerry and drank two neat whiskeys after the delicious dessert Calla put before them. Cade was so good to look at. He always had been, and the four years since he'd kissed her for the first time hadn't changed him very much on the surface. He was still overpoweringly masculine. Strong and capable and as tough as well-worn leather.

She watched the way his hands held the sheets of paper in their firm grip. They were tanned and sprinkled with dark hair. He didn't wear jewelry of any kind; the watch strapped around his wrist had a thick leather band and a dial that did everything except predict the future. He went in for utility, not style. But he managed to look like a fashion plate for all that, even in worn jeans and a faded shirt. He had a big, powerful body, and it was all steely muscle. Cade was just plain man, and he stood out anywhere.

He looked up once and caught her gaze, and she felt just a touch of the old magic. But she looked away and only the fear was left.

Later, Melly went into the bedroom with Abby. They sat on the old bed that had been Abby's from girlhood and went over the wedding dress pattern.

"It's just magnificent," Melly breathed. "But it will take forever for you to make it. . . ."

"A week, in my spare time." Abby grinned. "Do you really like it?"

"I love it!" She traced the design with a caressing finger. "It's the best design I've ever seen. You ought to sell it."

"Sell your wedding gown?" Abby exclaimed. "Do I look like I have a cash register for a heart?"

"Don't be silly. You know very well what I mean. It's good, Abby. It's really good. You're wasted showing other people's designs."

"Thank you for thinking so," Abby said with a smile.

"I'm not the only one, either. Did Jessica Dane ever get in touch with you?" Melly asked. "She absolutely raved over that dress you made me last summer."

"The boutique owner?" Abby asked. "No. Actually, I was kind of hoping she might. I do love designing, Melly. I feel as if modeling is burning me up. I stay tired all the time, and I have no social life at all. The money's nice," she added quietly. "But money isn't worth much in the long run if you aren't happy. And I'm not."

"Will you mind if I tell you that I never thought you would be?" her sister asked softly. She smiled. "You pretended it was what you wanted, but I saw right through you."

Abby stared at her ringless hands. "I hope nobody else did," she said.

"He's thirty-six now," Melly reminded her. "Inevitably, he'll marry sooner or later."

Abby laughed bitterly. "Will he? He hasn't exactly been in a flaming hurry to commit himself to anybody. You know what he used to say about marriage? That it was a noose only a fool stuck his head into."

"He's a lonely man, Abby," came the surprising reply. "I know better than anybody—I work for him. I see him every day. He works himself into the ground, but there are still evenings when he sits on the porch by himself and just stares off into the horizon."

That hurt. Abby turned her face away to keep Melly from seeing how much. "He could have any woman he wanted," she said, forcing herself not to let her voice show the emotion she was feeling. "He used to stay out with some woman or other every day I was here."

"So he let you think," Melly murmured. "He runs three ranches—a corporation the size of a small city—and in his spare time he sleeps. When does he have the time to be a playboy? I'll grant you, he's got the money to be one, even if he weren't so good-looking. But he's a puritan in his outlook. It even makes him uncomfortable when Jerry kisses me in front of him."

"Just like Donavan," she agreed, remembering Cade's father. "Remember the night you were kissing Danny Johnson on our front porch and Donavan rode by with Cade? Whew! I didn't think Danny would ever come back again after that lecture."

"Neither did I. Donavan had an overdeveloped sense of propriety. No wonder Cade's got so many inhibitions. Of course, being brought up in a small place like Cheyenne Lodge . . ."

"Only you could call Montana a small place," Abby teased.

"This little teeny corner of it, I meant," came the irrepressible reply. "I'll bet you get culture shock every time you come here from New York," she added.

"No," Abby denied. Her eyes began to glow softly. "It's like homecoming every time. I never realize how much I miss it until I come back."

"And stand at the window, hoping for a glimpse of Cade," Melly said quietly, nodding when Abby flushed. "Oh, yes, I've caught you at it. You watch him with such love in your eyes, Abby. As if the sight of him would sustain you through any nightmare."

Abby turned away. "Stop that. I'll wear my heart out on him, and you know it. No," she said firmly when Melly started to speak. "No more. Melly, you do love Jerry, don't you?" she added, concern replacing the brief flareup of irritation.

"Unbearably," Melly confessed. "We fought like animals the first few weeks I worked here, when I came home from business college. But then, one day he threw me down in the hay and fell on me," she added with a grin. "And we kissed like two starving lovers. He asked me to marry him on the spot and I said yes without even thinking. We've had our disagreements, but there's no one I'll ever love as much."

Abby thought about being pushed down and fallen on, and she trembled with reaction. She felt herself stiffen, and Melly noticed.

"Sorry," she said quickly, touching Abby's arm. "I didn't think about how it might sound to you."

"It's just the thought of being helpless," she said in a suppressed tone. Her eyes came up. "Melly, men are so strong . . . you don't realize how strong until you try to get away and can't!"

"Don't think about it," Melly said softly. "Come on, we've got to decide on the trimmings for this dress. Calla has a bag full of material samples she got from the fabric shop. We'll look through them, and she'll go into town and get what you need tomorrow, okay?"

"Okay." Abby hugged her warmly. "I love you," she said in a rare outburst of emotion.

"I love you, too," Melly returned, smiling as she drew away. "Now, here, this is what I liked especially. . . ." She pulled out a swatch of material and the girls drifted into a discussion of fabrics that lasted until bedtime.

Abby spent the next few days reacquainting herself with the ranch. She was careful to keep out of the way of the men—and Cade—but she trudged through the barns looking at calves and sat on the bales of hay in the loft and remembered back to her childhood on her family's ranch. It was part of Painted Ridge now, having been bought by Cade at Jesse Shane's death. It would have gone on the auction block otherwise, because neither Melly nor Abby had any desire to try to run it. Ranching was a fulltime headache, best left to experts.

When the snow melted and the weather turned springlike again, Abby wandered through the gates up to a grassy hill where a small stand of pines stood guard, and settled herself under one of the towering giants. It was good to breathe clean air, to sit and soak in the cool, green peace and untouched beauty of this land.

Where else were there still places like this, where you could look and see nothing but rolling grassy hills that stretched to the horizon—with tall, ragged mountains on the other side and the river that cut like a wide ribbon through it all? Cade had liked to fish in that river in the old days, when Donavan was still alive to assume some of the burden of their business. Abby went with him occasionally, watching him land big bass and crappie, rainbow trout and channel catfish.

The nice thing about Cade, she thought dreamily, was that he had such a love for the land and its protection. He was constantly investigating new ways of improving his own range, working closely with the Soil Conservation Service to protect the natural resources of his state.

Her eyes turned toward the gate as she heard a horse's hooves, and she found Cade riding up the ridge toward her on his big black gelding. He sat a horse so beautifully, reminding her of a Western movie hero. He was all muscle and grace, and she respected him more than any man she'd ever known.

He reined in when he reached her and swung one long leg around the pommel, a smoking cigarette in his lean, dark hands as he watched her from under the wide brim of his gray Stetson.

"Slumming, miss model?" he teased with a faint smile.

"This is the place for it," she said, leaning back against the tree to smile up at him. Her long, pale hair caught the breeze and curved around her flushed cheeks. "Isn't it peaceful here?" she asked. "No wonder the Indians fought so very hard to keep it."

His eyes darkened, narrowed. "A man does fight to keep the things he wants most," he said enigmatically, studying her. "Why do you wear those damned baggy things?" he demanded, nodding toward her bulky shirt and loose jeans.

She shrugged, avoiding that piercing gaze. "They're comfortable," she said inadequately.

"They look like hell. I'd rather see you in transparent blouses," he added coldly.

Her eyebrows arched. "You lecherous old thing," she accused.

He chuckled softly, deeply, a sound she hadn't heard in a long time. It made him seem younger. "Only with you, honey," he said softly. "I'm the soul of chivalry around most women."

Her eyes searched his. "You could have any woman you want these days," she murmured absently.

"Then isn't it a hell of a shame that I have such a fussy appetite?" he asked. He took a draw from the cigarette and studied her quietly. "I'm a busy man."

"You look it," she agreed, studying the dusty jeans that encased his hard, powerful legs, and his scuffed brown boots and sweat-stained denim shirt. There was a black mat of hair under that shirt, and a muscular chest that she remembered desperately wanting to touch.

"It's spring," he reminded her. "Cattle to doctor, calves to separate and brand and herds to move up to summer pasture as soon as we finish roundup. Hay to plant, machinery to repair and replace, temporary hands to hire for roundup, supplies to get in . . . if it isn't one damned thing, it's another."

"And you love every minute of it," she accused. "You'd die anywhere else."

"Amen." He finished the cigarette and tossed it down. "Crush that out for me, will you, honey?"

"It's not dry enough for it to cause a grass fire," she reminded him, but she got up and did it all the same.

"Back in the old days, Indians and white men would stop fighting to battle grass fires together," he told her with a grin. "They're still hard to stop, even today."

She looked up at him, tracing his shadowed face with eyes that ached for what might have been. "You look so at home in the saddle," she remarked.

"I grew up in it." He reached down an arm. "Step on my boot and come up here. I'll give you a ride home."

"It's a good thing you don't ride a horse the way you drive," she observed.

"That's not a good way to get reacquainted," he said shortly.

"It's only the truth. Donavan wouldn't even get in a truck with you," she reminded him. "Although I have to admit that you're a pretty good driver on the highway."

"Thanks for nothing. Are you coming or not?"

She wanted and dreaded the closeness. He was so very strong. What if she panicked again, what if he demanded an answer to her sudden nervousness?

"Abby," he said suddenly, his voice as full of authority as if he were tossing orders at his cowboys. "Come on."

She reacted to that automatically and took his hand, tingling as it slid up her arm to hold her. She stepped deftly onto the toe of his boot in the stirrup and swung up in front of him.

He drew her back against him with a steely arm, and she felt the powerful muscles of his chest at her shoulder blades.

"Comfortable?" he asked shortly.

"I'm fine," she replied in a voice that was unusually high-pitched.

He eased the horse into a canter. "You'll be more comfortable if you'll relax, little one," he murmured. "I'm no threat."

That was what he thought, she told herself, reacting wildly to the feel of his body against her back. He smelled of leather and cow and tobacco, and his breath sighed over her head, into her loosened hair.

If only she could relax instead of sitting like a fire poker in his light embrace. But he made her nervous, just as he always had; he made her feel vulnerable and soft and hungry. Despite the bad experience in New York, he appealed to her senses in ways that unnerved her.

He chuckled softly and she stiffened more. "What's so funny?" she muttered above the sound of the horse's hooves striking hard ground.

"You are. Should I be flattered that you're afraid to let me hold you on a horse? My God, I didn't realize I was so devastating at close range. Or," he added musingly, "is it that I smell like a man who's been working with cattle?"

Laughter bubbled up inside her. It had been years since she and Cade had spent any time alone, and she'd forgotten his dry sense of humor.

"Sorry." She sighed. "I've been away longer than I realized."

His big arm tightened for an instant and relaxed, and she let him hold her without a struggle. His strength was less intimidating now than it had been the last time, as if the nightmare experience were truly fading away in the scope and bigness of this country where she had grown up. She felt safe. Safer than she'd felt in years.

"Four years," he murmured behind her head. "Except for a few days here and there, when you could tear yourself away from New York."

She went taut with indignation. "Are you going to start that again?"

"I never stopped it. You just stopped listening." His arm contracted impatiently for an instant, and his warm breath was on her ear. "When are you going to grow up, Abby? Glitter isn't enough for a lifetime. In the end, it's not going to satisfy you as a woman!"

"What is?" she asked curtly. "Living with some man and raising children?"

He seemed to freeze, as if she'd thrown cold water in his face, and she was sorry she'd said that. She hadn't meant it—she was just getting back at him.

"It's more than enough for women out here," he said shortly.

She stared across at the horizon, loving the familiar contours of the land, the shape of the tall trees, the blueness of the sky. "Your grandmother had ten children, didn't she, Cade?" she asked, remembering the photos in the McLaren family album.

"Yes." He laughed shortly. "There wasn't much choice in those days, honey. Women didn't have a lot of control over their bodies, like they do now."

"And it took big families to run ranches and farms," she agreed. She leaned back against him, feeling his muscles ripple with the motion of the horse. Her eyes closed as she drank in the sensation of being close.

"It was more than that," he remarked as they approached the house. "People in love want children."

She laughed aloud at that. "I can't imagine you in love," she said. "It's completely out of character. What was it you always said about never letting a woman put a ring through your nose?"

He didn't laugh. If anything, he seemed to grow cold. "You don't know me at all, Abby. You never have."

"Who could get close enough?" she asked coolly. "You've got a wall ten feet thick around yourself, just like Donavan had. It must be a McLaren trait."

"When people come close, they can hurt," he said shortly. "I've had my fill of being cut to the quick."

"I can't imagine anyone brave enough to try that," she told him.

"Can't you?" He sounded goaded, and the arm that was holding her tautened.

She got a glimpse of his face as he leaned down to open the gate between them and the house, and its hardness unsettled her. He looked hurt somehow, and she couldn't understand why.

"Cade?" she murmured before he straightened again.

His eyes looked straight into hers, and she trembled at the intensity of the glare, its suppressed violence.

"One day, you'll push too hard," he said quietly. "I'm not made of stone, despite the fact that you seem to believe I am. I let you get away with murder when you were younger. But you're not a child anymore, Abby, and the kid gloves are off. Do you understand me?"

How could she help it? Her heart shuddered with mingled fear and excitement. Involuntarily, her eyes went to his hard mouth and she remembered vividly the touch and taste and expertness of it.

"Don't worry, Cade, I won't seduce you," she promised, trying to sound as if she were teasing him in a sophisticated way.

He caught her chin and forced her eyes back up to his, and she jumped at the ferocity in his dark gaze. "I could have had you that night at the swimming pool, Abigail Jennifer Shane," he reminded her with merciless bluntness. "We're both four years older, but don't think you're immune to me. If you start playing games, you could goad me into doing something we'd both regret."

She tried to breathe normally and failed miserably. She forced her eyes down to the harsh rise and fall of his chest, and then closed them.

"Just because I had a huge crush on you once,

don't get conceited and think I'm still stupid enough to moon over you, Cade," she bit off.

As if the words set him off, his eyes flashed and all at once he had her across the saddle, over his knees, with her head imprisoned in the crook of his arm.

She struggled, frightened by his strength as she'd been afraid from the beginning that she would be. "No," she whispered, pushing frantically at his chest.

"Let's see how conceited I am, Abby," he ground out, bending his head to hers.

One glance into those blazing eyes was enough to tell her that he wasn't teasing. She groaned helplessly as his hard mouth crushed down onto hers in cold, angry possession.

It might have been so different if he'd been careful, if he hadn't given in to his temper. But she was too frightened to think rationally. It was New York all over again, and a man's strength was holding her helpless while a merciless mouth ground against her own. Through the fear, she thought she felt Cade tremble, but she couldn't be sure. Her mind was focused only on the hard pressure of his mouth, the painful tightening of his arms. Suddenly she began to fight. She hit him with her fists, anywhere she could, and when the shock of it made him lift his head, she screamed.

An indescribable expression washed over his features, and he seemed to go pale.

Abby hung back against his arm, her pale brown eyes full of terror, her lips bloodless as she stared up at him, her breasts rising and falling with her strangled breaths.

"My God, what's happened to you?" he asked in a shocked undertone.

She swallowed nervously, her lips trembling with reaction, her body frozen in its arch. "Please . . . don't handle me . . . roughly," she pleaded, her voice strange and high.

His eyes narrowed, glittering. His face went rock hard as he searched her features. "What made you come here, Abby?" he demanded. "What drove you out of the city?"

Her eyes closed and she shuddered. "I told you, I was tired," she choked out. "Tired!"

He said something terrible under his breath and straightened, moving her away from him with a smooth motion. "It's all right," he said when her eyes flew open at the movement. "I'm only going to let you sit up."

She avoided his piercing scrutiny, sitting quickly erect with her back to him.

He spurred the horse toward the house. "If you can't bear to be touched, there has to be a reason," he said shortly. "You've been hurt some way, or frightened. I asked you if you'd been knocked around by a man, and you denied it. But you lied to me, didn't you, Abby?"

Her jaw set firmly. "All this fuss because you kissed me against my will and I fought you!" she burst out. "Are you so conceited that you think I can't wait to fall into your arms, Cade?"

He didn't say a word. He rode right up to the front steps and abruptly set her down on the ground.

She stood by the horse for a long moment before she looked up. "Thanks for the ride," she ventured.

He'd lit a cigarette and was smoking it quietly, his

face grim as he looked down at her. "You're going to tell me what happened sooner or later."

"Nothing happened," she lied, raising her voice.

"I didn't wind up with three ranches and a corporation because I was an idiot," he informed her. "You didn't come rushing down here a month early just to help Melly get ready for her wedding. And it damned sure wasn't because you were dying for the sight of me."

He was hitting too close to the truth. She turned away. "Believe what you like, Great White Rancher."

"Abby!"

She whirled, eyes blazing, as gloriously beautiful in anger as a sunburst, with her pale hair making a frame for her delicate face and wide brown eyes. "What?"

His eyes went over her reverently, from toes to head, while the cigarette smoked away in his tanned fingers. "Don't fight me."

It was like having the breath knocked out of her. She looked up at him and felt the anger drain away. He was so gorgeously masculine, so handsome. Her eyes softened helplessly.

"Then don't hurt me," she said quietly.

He laughed mirthlessly. "That works both ways."

"Pull the other one," she muttered. "I'd have to use dynamite. You're hard, Cade."

"This is hard country. I don't have time for the limp-wristed courtesies you city women swear by in men."

"Sophistication doesn't make a man peculiar," she returned. "I like a polished man."

His dark eyes glittered. "Not always," he replied.

"There was a time when I could look at you and make you blush."

"That old crush?" she said. "I thought the sun rose and set on you, all right. But you made a career of pushing me away, didn't you?"

"You were eighteen, damn it!" he shot at her. "Eighteen, to my thirty-two! I felt like a damned fool when I left you that night. I should never have touched you!"

The one beautiful memory in her life, and he was sorry it had happened. If she'd ever wondered how he really felt inside his shell, she knew now.

She lowered her eyes and turned away. She walked to the house without another word, without a backward glance. As she went up the steps, she imagined she heard him swear, but when she looked back, he was riding away.

Abby brooded about the confrontation for the rest of the day, and at the supper table it was patently obvious to Melly and Jerry that something was wrong. Even Calla, walking back and forth to serve up the delicious beef the ranch was famous for with the accompanying dishes, commented that the weather sure had gotten cold quick.

Cade finished his meal before the rest of them and lit a cigarette over his second cup of coffee.

"I've got those reports printed out whenever you want them, Cade," Melly ventured.

He nodded. "I'll look them over now. Jerry, come on in when you finish," he added, rising. "We'll have to make a decision pretty quick about those cows we're going to sell off. Jake White wants a few dozen head for embryo transplants."

"Wants them cheap, too." Jerry laughed. "I reckon he thinks our culls will be the very thing to carry his purebred Angus."

Melly grinned at them, aware of Abby sitting rigidly at her side. "Oh, the advances in cattle breeding. Herefords throwing Angus calves, without even the joys of natural conception."

Cade gave her a hard glare and walked out of the room.

"Shame on you," Jerry muttered as he started to join the boss. "Embarrassing him that way."

"I'm just helping him lose some of his inhibitions, darling," Melly whispered back, blowing him a kiss before he winked and left the room.

"He'll get even," Abby said solemnly, picking at her food. "He always does."

"You could help him with those inhibitions, too," her sister said, tongue in cheek.

"Not me, sis," came the instant reply. She glared toward the doorway. "He can keep his hangups for all I care."

Melly stared at her hard. "Why don't you and Cade start kissing and stop fighting?"

"Ask him," she grumbled, getting up. "It's one and the same thing with Cade, if you want to know. I've got a frightful headache, Melly. Say goodnight to the others for me, will you?" And she rushed upstairs without another word before Melly could ask the questions that were forming on her lips.

Abby hadn't had a nightmare since she arrived at

the ranch, but after the confrontation with Cade, it was almost inevitable that it would recur. And sure enough, it did.

She woke up in the early hours of the morning, screaming. Even as the sounds were dying away, her door burst open and Cade came storming into her room, flashing on the overhead light, with Melly at his heels.

6

Abby sat there in the plain cotton gown that concealed every inch of her body, her hair wild, her eyes raining tears down her pale cheeks, and gaped at them on the tail of terror.

Cade was in his pajama trousers and nothing else. They rode low on his lean hips, and the sheer masculinity of his big body with its generous black, curling hair and bronzed muscle was enough to frighten her even more.

"How about making some coffee?" Cade asked Melly, although his tone made it an order, not a request.

"But . . ." Melly began, nervously looking from her sister to her employer.

"You heard me."

Melly hesitated for just an instant before she left them alone, her footsteps dying away down the hall.

Cade put his hands on his hips and stared down at

Abby. With his hair tousled and his face hard, he looked as threatening as any storm.

"Get up and put on a robe," he said after a minute, turning away, "while I get dressed."

"You don't have to," she managed weakly.

He half turned, his eyes glittering. "Don't I?" he growled. "You're looking at me as if I were a rapist."

Her face blanched and he nodded. "That's how you feel, too, isn't it, baby? Put on a robe and come into the living room. And stop looking at me like that. I'm not going to touch you. But you're going to tell me the truth, one way or the other."

He left her sitting there, his back as stiff as a poker.

Melly brought the coffee in just as Abby came out of her room, wrapped to the throat in a heavy navy terrycloth robe.

Cade was dressed, barely, in jeans and an open-throated blue shirt that he hadn't tucked in. He was barefoot, sitting forward in an armchair, worrying his hair with his hands. He looked up as Abby came in.

"Sit down," he said quietly. "Melly, thank you for the coffee. Goodnight."

"Cade . . ." Melly began.

"Goodnight," he repeated.

The younger woman sighed as she looked over at Abby, her whole expression one of regret and apology.

"It's all right," Abby said gently. "You and I both know that Cade would never hurt me."

Cade looked faintly shocked by the words, but he busied himself with lighting a cigarette while Melly said goodnight and left them alone.

"Fix me a cup, will you, honey?" he asked.

Abby automatically poured cream in it and handed it to him.

He took it, cup and saucer balanced on his big palm, and smiled at her. "You remembered, didn't you?"

She flushed. Yes, she had, just the way he liked it. She remembered almost everything she'd learned over the years—that he didn't take sugar, that he hated rhubarb, that he loved a thick steak and cottage potatoes to go with it, that he could go for forty-eight hours without sleep but not one hour without a cigarette . . .

"Tit for tat?" he murmured, and reached out to put two sugars and cream in the second cup and hand it to her, smiling when she raised astonished eyes to his.

She took it, sitting back on the sofa to study the creamy liquid, turning the cup nervously back and forth in its saucer.

"Little things," she murmured, finally lifting her eyes to his. "Isn't it amazing how we remember them after so many years?"

"I remember a lot about you," he said quietly, studying her. "Especially," he added on a rueful sigh, "how you look without clothes."

She flushed, dropping her eyes. "It was a long time ago."

"Four years," he agreed. "But it doesn't seem that long to me." He took a gulp of his coffee, ignoring the fact that it was hot enough to blister a normal throat, stubbed out his cigarette and leaned back in his chair. "Tell me what happened, Abby."

She felt the cup tremble in her hand and only just righted it in time. "I can't, Cade."

He took another sip of coffee and leaned forward suddenly, resting his hands on his knees. "Look up. That's right, look at me. Do you remember when you ran over your father's dog with my old jeep?"

She swallowed and nodded.

"You couldn't face him, but you came running to me bawling your heart out, and I held you while you cried." He shifted his hands, studying her drawn face. "When Vennie Walden called you a tomboy and said you looked like a stick with bumps, you came crying to me then."

She nodded again, managing a smile for him. "I always cried on you, didn't I?"

"Always. Why not now?" He reached out a big hand and waited, patiently, until she could put her own, hesitantly, into it and feel its warmth and strength. "From now on, it's going to be just like this. I won't touch you unless you want me to. Now tell me what happened. Did you find out he was married?"

"He?" she asked, studying him blankly.

"The man you had an affair with," he said quietly. "The one you wake up screaming over in the middle of the night."

She swallowed down the urge to get up and run. How in the world was she going to be able to tell him the truth. How?!

"Come on, Abby, tell me," he coaxed with a faint smile. "I'm not going to sit in judgment on you."

"You've got it wrong, Cade," she said after a minute. "It . . . wasn't an affair."

His heavy brows came together. He searched her face. "No? I understood Melly to say there was a man. . . ."

"There was." Her eyes opened and closed, and the pain of admission was in them suddenly. She tried to speak, and her mouth trembled on the words.

He was beginning to sense something. His face seemed to darken, his eyes glittered. His hand, on hers, tightened promptingly. "Abby, tell me!" he ground out, his patience exhausted.

Her eyes closed, because she couldn't bear to see what would be in his when she told him. "I was assaulted, Cade."

The silence seemed to go on forever. Forever! The hand around her own stilled, and withdrew. Somewhere a clock was ticking with comical loudness; she could hear it above the tortured pounding of her own heart. . . .

At first, she wondered if he'd heard her. Until she looked up and saw his lean hands, tough from years of ranch work, contract slowly around the cup until it shattered and coffee went in a half-dozen directions onto the deep grey pile carpet.

Her eyes shot up to his face, reading the aching compassion and murderous rage that passed across it in wild succession.

"Who?" he asked, the word dangerously soft.

"I don't know," she said quietly.

"Surely to God there was a suspect!" he burst out, oblivious to the shards of pottery and the coffee that was staining his jeans, the carpet.

"Not yet," she told him. "Cade, the carpet . . . look, you've cut your hand!" she exclaimed, seeing blood.

"Oh, to hell with that," he growled. He glanced at his hand and tugged a handkerchief from his jeans pocket to wind haphazardly around it. "What do you mean, not yet?"

"Just what I said. It's a big city." She got up, kneeling beside him. "Let me see. Come on, let me see!" she grumbled, forcing him to give her the big, warm hand. She unwrapped the handkerchief gently; there was a shallow cut on the ball of his thumb. "We'd better put something on it."

"Is that why you backed away from me earlier?" he asked, his eyes on her bent head. "Why you were afraid when I was rough with you earlier, outside?"

Her eyes closed. "Yes."

He started to touch her hair and froze, withdrawing his hand before it could make contact. He laid it back on the arm of the chair with a wistful sigh. "What can I say, Abby?" he asked gently. "What in hell can I say?"

Her fingers let go of his hand and she got to her feet. "There's some antiseptic in the guest bathroom, isn't there?" she asked.

"I suppose so." He got up and followed her down the hall, sitting uncomfortably on the little vanity bench, which swayed precariously while she riffled through the medicine cabinet for antiseptic and a bandage.

He sat quietly while she dressed the cut, but his eyes watched her intently.

"Please don't watch me like that," she asked tightly.

His eyes fell to his hand. "It's an old habit." His chiseled mouth made a half-smile when she looked down at him, startled. "You didn't know that, I suppose." The smile faded. "Can you talk about it?"

She studied him quietly and lowered her eyes. "I was coming home from an assignment, at night. It was a nice night, just a little nippy, and I had a coat on over my dress. I only lived a few blocks away, so I walked." She laughed bitterly. "The streets were deserted, and before I realized it, a man started following me. I ran, and he caught up with me and dragged me into an alley." She shuddered at the memory. "I tried so hard to get away, but he was big and terribly strong. . . ." Her eyes closed. "He pushed me down and started kissing me, touching me . . . I screamed then, just as loud as I could, and there were three men coming out of a nearby bar who heard me. They came running and he took off." She drew in a steadying breath, oblivious to Cade's white, strained face. "Thank God, they heard me. People talk about cities being cold and heartless places, but it didn't happen that way for me. The people at the emergency room told me I'd been damned lucky."

"Was there someone to take care of you?" he asked as if it mattered, really mattered.

"Yes. There was a Rape Crisis Center. All women," she said with a faint smile, recalling the gentle treatment, the care she'd received. "They sent me over there, despite the fact that I hadn't been raped. It's still a mentally scarring thing, to be handled that way, mauled. Thinking about the way it might have been . . . but I felt dirty, you know. Soiled. I still think about it constantly. . . ."

His face hardened as he watched her quietly. "If I'd made love to you that night, kept you here with me, none of this would ever have happened."

"Did you want to, really?" she wondered softly.

He drew in a long, steady breath. "I wanted to," he admitted after a minute, and his eyes darkened. He got to his feet, towering over her. "But it would have been a slap in the face to your father. He trusted me to look after you. And God knows, it would have been a mistake, a bad one." He studied her intently. "I'd never touched a virgin until that night."

She felt a surge of pride at that confession, and it showed in her eyes.

"I've never touched one since, either," he added with a quiet smile.

"Learned your lesson, huh?" she murmured with a feeble attempt at humor.

He nodded. "Can you sleep now?"

The thought of the dark room was disquieting, but she erased the nervousness from her eyes. "Yes. I think so."

"You can sleep with me if you want to," he said quietly, and she knew exactly what he meant—that he'd die before he'd touch her, unless she wanted it.

Hesitantly, her hand went out to touch his arm, a light touch that was quickly removed. "Thank you," she said softly. "But I'll be all right now."

His eyes searched hers for a long moment. "You trust me, don't you?" he asked gently.

"Yes," she said simply. "More than anyone else in the world, Cade, if it means anything."

"Yes," he bit off, "it means something."

"The carpet!" she exclaimed suddenly. "Oh, Cade, I'll bet the carpet's ruined. . . ."

"I'll buy a new one. Go to bed."

"Thank you," she said as he turned to go out into the hall. "I . . . I . . . Melly said I should have told you about it, but I didn't . . . I wasn't sure. . . ."

"You didn't think that I'd blame you?" he asked softly.

She stared down at the carpeted floor, embarrassed now that he knew.

"Stop it, for God's sake," he said bluntly. "So you got mauled. You've had a terrible experience, and I'm sorry as hell, but it doesn't change who you are!"

Her lips trembled. "I feel unclean," she whispered, shaken. "As if I'd been robbed of something I had the right to give to a man I chose. He touched me in ways no man ever did, not even you . . ."

He drew in a ragged breath. "Yes, you were robbed, but not of your chastity. Even if he'd raped you, you'd still have that."

She stared up at him numbly. "What?"

He lit a cigarette with unsteady fingers. "Oh, hell, I'm putting this badly." He blew out a cloud of smoke and stared down at her with narrowed eyes. "Abby, how long ago did it happen?"

"Week before last," she confessed.

"Okay, and you're still raw, that makes sense. But you'll get over it. And it will be different, with a man you care about."

Her lips pouted. "It wasn't any different this afternoon. You scared me to death."

His face paled, but he didn't look away. "My fault. I've been without a woman for a while, and the feel of you went to my head. I was rougher than I ever meant to be. But you've got to help yourself a little by not dwelling on what happened to you."

"How can I help it? It makes me sick just remembering . . . !" she burst out.

"Put it in perspective, honey," he said curtly, jamming his bandaged hand in his pocket as if he were afraid he might try to touch her with it. "Has it occurred to you that by letting the experience warp your mind, you're giving that piece of scum who attacked you more rights over you than you'd give a husband?"

She stared at him, stunned.

He took another long draw from the cigarette. "You're giving him the right to dominate your life, by dwelling on what happened, by blowing up what he did to you and letting it lock you up emotionally and physically."

"I . . . hadn't thought of it like that."

"Suppose you start."

She wrapped her arms around her trembling body. "You can't know how it is for a woman," she murmured. "Against a man's strength . . ."

"I can remember a time in your life when you very much liked being helpless against mine," he said under his breath.

"That was different. I knew you'd never hurt me."

"You knew that this afternoon, but you fought me like a wildcat."

She flushed. "You hurt me!"

His jaw tightened. "Do you think because I have to be hard with my men that I'm that hard inside? You get under my skin like no other woman ever has. You deliberately needle me and then take offense when I defend myself. It's always been that way."

"I never thought you could be hurt," she murmured, avoiding his piercing gaze. "Least of all by me."

"Why talk about it?" he asked wearily. "It's all water under the bridge now."

"Thanks for the therapy session," she said softly and smiled, because she meant it.

He smiled back. "Did it help?"

She nodded. Her eyes searched his. "Cade, I'm sorry I screamed this afternoon."

He reached down and smoothed a lock of hair from her face. "I didn't know. Now I do. Give it time—you'll be fine. I'll help."

"Thanks for letting me come."

He looked strange for a minute. "When Melly said you wanted to get here early for the wedding, so you could spend some time on the ranch, I didn't know the real reason. I thought . . ." He dropped his hand with a gruff laugh. "You can still sleep with me, if you want. I wouldn't touch you."

Her soft eyes searched his, and he looked back as if it were beyond his power to remove his eyes from hers. "Calla and Melly would be shocked to the back teeth," she whispered, trying to joke about it and failing. It would have been heaven to lie in his arms all night. "But thank you for the offer."

He shrugged. "It wasn't for purely selfless reasons," he said, winking at her. "Bed's damned cold in early spring," he chuckled.

She hit him softly. "Beast!"

"Think you can sleep now?"

She nodded. "I feel a little different about it. Maybe I just need time to put things into perspective after all."

"If you'd like something to occupy your mind, I'll take you out to see the rest of the calves in the morning."

"Oh, boy," she said enthusiastically. "But what if it snows again?" she asked. "It was awfully cloudy this afternoon and cold as blazes and the radio says—"

"When has snow ever stopped me?" he asked, chuckling. "Night, honey." He turned and strode off toward the stairs.

When has anything ever stopped you? she asked herself silently.

Except once . . . she'd never realized until now that he'd really wanted her that night. He'd been so cool and calm on the surface that she'd halfway convinced herself he had only been satisfying her curiosity to keep her from experimenting with younger, more hot-blooded males. But now she began to wonder. She was still wondering when she fell into a deep, satisfying sleep.

7

Cade had offered to take Abby back to see the calves, but by morning the snow had covered Painted Ridge and he was out with his men trying to bring in the half-frozen calves and their new mothers. According to Hank, Cade was cursing a blue streak from one end of the ranch to the other.

"Wants his other gloves," Hank growled at Calla when he paused in the hall, the familiar wad of tobacco tucked into his cheek. "Ruined a pair trying to unhook one of them damned cows from the barbed wire."

"He goes through gloves like some men go through food," Calla grumbled, shooting an irritated glance at Hank for interrupting her in the middle of lunch preparation. "Only got one pair left as it is. You best remember to tell him that!"

"Can't tell him a damned thing," Hank muttered, waiting uncomfortably in the hall. His wide-brimmed hat was spotted with melted snow, and his heavy cloth coat was equally damp. "He hit the ground cussing this morning and he ain't stopped yet. I just follow orders, I don't give 'em!" he shouted after Calla.

"Is it bad out there?" Melly called from the den, where she was busily operating Cade's computer.

"Bad enough," Hank replied. "Hope your fingers are rested, Miss Melly, 'cause you're sure going to do some typing when we get a tally on these new calves!"

"As usual." Melly laughed. "Don't worry about it, Hank, I get paid good."

"If we got paid what we was worth, Cade would go in the hole, I guess," the thin cowboy said to no one in particular. He glanced at Abby, who was standing there quietly in her jeans and a blue turtleneck sweater. "I hear you're going to stay with us till Miss Melly's wedding. How're you settling in?"

She smiled. "Just fine. It feels like old times."

"Far cry from the city," he observed.

She nodded. "Less traffic," she said with a hint of her old humor.

Hank looked disgusted. "Give me a horse any day," he muttered, "and open country to ride him in. If God wanted the world covered in concrete, he'd have made human beings with tires!"

It was the cowboy's favorite theme, and Abby was looking for a way to escape before he had time to get started when Calla came thumping back down the hall with a worn pair of gloves in her hand.

"Here," she said shortly, slapping them into Hank's outstretched hand. "And make sure he doesn't get holes in them. That's all there is."

"What am I, a nursemaid?" he spat out. "My gosh, Calla, all I do is babysit cows these days. If Cade gave a hang about my feelings, he'd give me some decent work."

"Maybe he'll set you to digging post holes," the older woman suggested with malicious glee. "I'll tell him what you said."

"You do," he threatened, "and I'll tell him what you did with that cherry cake he had his heart set on the other night."

She sucked in a furious breath. "You wouldn't dare!"

He grinned, something rare for Hank. "You tell him I like digging post holes, and I'll do it or bust. Bye, Abby, Melly," he called over his shoulder as he stomped out the door.

"What did you do with Cade's cherry cake?" Abby asked with a sideways stare.

Calla cleared her throat and walked back toward the kitchen. "I gave it to Jeb. Cade's not the only one who's partial to my cherry cake."

Abby smothered a chuckle as she wandered into the den. With its bare wood floors, Indian rugs and wood furniture, it was a far cry from the luxury of the living room.

Melly looked up as Abby came toward the desk where the computer and printer were set up. "I didn't want to desert you last night," she said apologetically. "Did you tell him?"

"I had to," Abby admitted, perching herself on the edge of the chair beside Melly's. "You know Cade when he sets his mind on something. But it wasn't as bad as I thought it would be. He didn't even say 'I told you so.' "

"I didn't expect him to. You underestimate him sometimes, I think." Melly looked smug. "There's a brown spot on the carpet in the living room."

Abby looked guilty. "I was afraid of that, but he wouldn't hear of my cleaning it up." She sighed. "He was holding the coffee cup when I told him. He . . . crushed it."

Melly closed her eyes for an instant. "I noticed his hand was bandaged this morning," she murmured. "I wondered why. . . ."

"He said some things that made me think," Abby recalled, smiling faintly. "He may not be a psychologist, but he's got a lot of common sense about things. He said I was giving the man who attacked me a hold over me, by dwelling on it. I'd never considered it in that light, but I think he has a point."

Melly smiled at her gently. "Maybe he ought to open an office," she said impishly.

Abby grinned back. "Maybe he ought." She studied her sister closely for a minute as her head bent over the computer keyboard while she typed in a code and glanced up at the screen. The abbreviations were Greek to Abby, but they seemed to make sense to Melly.

"What are you doing?"

"Herd records. We're getting ready to cull cattle, you know. Any cows that don't come up to par are going to be sold off, especially if they aren't producing enough calves or if the ones they're producing aren't good enough or if they're old. . . ."

"Slavery," Abby burst out. "Horrible!"

Melly laughed merrily. "Yes, Cade was telling me what you thought about veal smothered in onions."

"That's really horrible," she muttered. "Poor little thing, all cold and half-frozen and its mama turned her back on it, and Cade talks about eating it. . . ."

"Life goes on, darling," Melly reminded her, "and a cattle ranch is no place for sentiment. I can just see you owning one—you'd make pets of all the cattle and become a vegetarian."

"Hmmm," Abby said, frowning thoughtfully, "I wonder if Cade's ever thought of that?"

"I don't know," came the amused reply, "but if I were you, I'd wait until way after roundup to ask him!"

Abby laughed. "You may have a point."

Melly murmured something, but her mind went quickly back to the computer and her work. Abby, curious, asked questions and Melly told her about the computer network between Cade's ranches, and the capacity of the computer for storing information about the cattle. There was even a videocassette setup so that Cade could sell cattle to people who had never been to the ranch to see them—they could buy from the tape. He could buy the same way, by watching film of a bull he was interested in, for example. It was a far cry from the old days of ranching when ranchers kept written records and went crazy trying to keep up with thousands of head of cattle. Abby was fascinated by the computer and the rapidity of its operation. But after a few minutes the phone started ringing and didn't stop, and Abby wandered off to watch the snow.

"Isn't Cade going to come in and eat?" Melly asked

as Calla set a platter of ham and bread and condiments on the table, along with a plate of homemade french fries.

"Nope." The older woman sighed. "Said to pack him a sandwich and a thermos of coffee and he'd run up to the house to get it." She nodded toward a sack and a thermos on the buffet.

"Is he coming right up?" Abby asked.

"Any minute."

"I'll carry it out," Abby volunteered, and grabbed it up, hurrying toward the front door. She only paused long enough to tug on galoshes and her thick cloth coat, and rushed out onto the porch as she heard a pickup skid up to the house and stop.

Cade was sitting in the cab when she crunched her way through the blowing snow to the truck. He threw open the passenger door.

"Thanks, honey," he said, taking the sack and thermos from her and placing them on the seat beside him. "Get in out of the snow."

She started to close the truck door, but he shook his head. "In here," he corrected. "With me."

Something about the way he said it made her pulse pound, and she shook herself mentally. She was reading things into his deep voice, that was all.

"Hank said you were turning the air blue. Is this new snow your fault?" Abby asked him with humor in her pale brown eyes.

He returned the smile and there was a light in his eyes she hadn't noticed before. "I reckon," he murmured, watching the color come and go in her flushed face. "Feel better this morning?"

"Yes, thank you," she said softly.

He reached out a big hand and held it, palm up.

She hesitated for an instant before she reached out her own cold, slender hand and put it gingerly into his. The hard fingers closed softly around it and squeezed.

"This is how it's going to be from now on," he said, his voice deep and quiet, the two of them isolated in the cold cab while feathery snow fell onto the windshield, the hood, the landscape. "I'll ask, I won't take."

She looked into his eyes and felt, for a second, the old magic of electricity between them. "That goes against the grain, I'll bet," she said.

"I'm used to taking," he replied. "But I can get used to asking, I suppose. How about you?"

She looked down at his big hand swallowing hers, liking the warmth and strength of it even while something in the back of her mind rebelled at that strength. "I don't know," she said honestly.

"What frightens you most?" he asked.

"Your strength," she said, without taking time to think, and her eyes came up to his.

He nodded, and not by a flicker of an eyelash did he betray any emotion beyond curiosity. "And if I let you make all the moves?" he asked quietly. "If I let you come close or touch or hold, instead of moving in on you?"

The thought fascinated her. That showed in her unblinking gaze, in the slight tilt of her head.

"Therapy, Cade?" she asked in a soft, steady tone.

"Whatever name you want to call it." He opened his hand so that she could leave hers there or remove it, as she wished. It was more than a gesture—it was a statement.

She smiled slowly. "Such power might go to my head," she said with a tentative laugh. "Suppose I decided to have my way with you?" she added, finding that she could treat the matter lightly for the moment.

He cocked an eyebrow and looked stern. "Don't start getting any ideas about me. I'm not easy. None of you wild city girls are going to come out here and lure me into any haystacks."

She let her fingers curl into his and hold them. "It's a long shot," she said after a minute.

"My grandfather won this ranch in a poker game in Cheyenne," he remarked. "I guess it's in my blood to take long shots."

"Won't it interfere with your private life?" she added, hoping her question wouldn't sound as if she were fishing.

He studied her closely for a minute before he replied. "I thought you knew that I don't have affairs."

She almost jumped at the quiet intensity of his eyes. "I . . . never really thought about it," she lied.

"I've had women," he said, "but nothing permanent, nothing lasting. There's no private life for you to interfere with."

She was suddenly fiercely glad of that, although she didn't know how to tell him. "It's not going to be very easy," she confessed shyly. "I've never been forward, even before this happened."

"I know," he murmured, smiling down at her. "I could sit here and look at you all day," he said after a minute, "but it wouldn't get the work done," he added ruefully.

"I could come and help you," she volunteered, wondering at her sudden reluctance to leave him.

"It's too cold, honey," he said. His eyes wandered over her soft, flushed face. "Feel like kissing me?"

Her heart jumped. She felt a new kind of excitement at the thought of it. "I thought you weren't easy," she challenged as she slid hesitantly toward him.

Surprise registered in his eyes, but only for a second. "Well, only with some girls," he corrected, smiling wickedly. "Come on, hurry up, I've got calves to deliver."

"Young Dr. McLaren," she murmured, looking up at him from close range, seeing new lines in his face, fatigue in his dark eyes. There were a few silver hairs over his temples and she touched them with unsteady fingers. "You're going grey, Cade."

"I got those because of you, when you were in your early teens," he reminded her. "Hanging off saddles trying to do trick riding, falling into the rapids out of a rickety canoe, flying over fences trying to ride Donavan's broncs . . . my God, you were a handful!"

"Well, Melly and I didn't have a mama," she reminded him, "and Dad was in poor health from the time we got in grammar school on. If it hadn't been for you and Calla and the cowboys, I guess Melly and I wouldn't have made it."

"Stop that," he growled. "And don't make me out to be an old man. I'm just fourteen years older than you, and I never did feel like a relative."

She put her fingers against his warm lips and felt their involuntary pursing with a tingle of satisfaction. "I didn't mean it that way." She looked into his dark eyes with a thrill of pure pleasure. "Can I really kiss you?"

His chest seemed to rise and fall with unusual rapidity; his nostrils flared under heavy breaths. "Do you want to?"

"I . . . I want to." She reached around his neck to pull his dark head down to hers, letting her fingers savor the thick coolness of his hair. Her eyes fell to his hard lips and she noticed that they didn't part when hers touched them, as if he were keeping himself on a tight rein to prevent the kiss from becoming intimate.

She liked the warmth of his mouth under hers, and she liked the faint rasp of his cheek where her nose rubbed against it as she pressed harder against his lips. His breath was even harder now but he wasn't moving a muscle. With a quiet, trusting sigh she eased away from him and looked up.

His face was rigid, his eyes blazing back at her. "Okay?" she asked uncertainly, needing reassurance.

A faint smile softened his expression. "Okay."

She frowned slightly, studying his set lips. "You kept your mouth closed, though," she said absently.

"I don't think we need to go that far that fast, baby," he said quietly.

He moved away from her, his hand going to the ignition to start the truck and let it idle. "It's like learning to walk. You have to do it one step at a time."

"That was a nice step," she told him with a smile.

"I thought so myself." He raised his chin and his

eyes were all arrogance. "Are you going to need an engraved invitation every time from now on?"

"I guess I could sneak up on your blind side," she confessed with a grin. "Or drag you off into dark corners. Maybe if I watch Melly and Jerry I'll get some new ideas. She said he pushed her into a hay stall and fell on her."

He burst out laughing, and she found that she could laugh, too—a far cry from her first reaction when Melly had confessed it.

"That sounds like Jerry," he said after a minute. His eyes searched hers. "It's what I'd have done, once."

The smile faded, and she felt a deep sadness for what might have been if she hadn't been so crazy to go to New York and break into modeling.

"In a hay stall?" she teased halfheartedly.

"Anywhere. As long as it was with you, and I could feel you . . . all of you . . . under my body."

She turned away from the hunger in his eyes with a tiny little sound, and he hit the steering wheel with his hand and stared blindly out the windshield, cursing under his breath.

"I'm sorry," he ground out. "That was a damned stupid thing to say . . . !"

"Don't handle me with kid gloves," she said, looking back at him. "Melly was right, and so were you. I can't run away from the memory of the attack, and I can't run away from life. I'm going to have to learn to deal with . . . relationships, physical relationships." Her eyes met his bravely. "Help me."

"I've already told you that I will."

She studied the worn mat on the floorboard. "And don't get angry when I react . . . predictably."

"Like just now?" he asked, and managed a smile.

She nodded, smiling back. "Like just now." Her eyes searched his, looking for reassurance. "It frightens me, still, the . . . the weight of a man's body," she whispered shakily, and only realized much later that she'd confessed that to no one else.

"In that case," he said gently, "I'll have to let you push me down in the hay, won't I?"

Tears misted in her eyes. "Oh, Cade . . ."

"Will you get out of my truck?" he asked pleasantly, preventing her, probably intentionally, from showing any gratitude. "I think I did mention about a half-hour ago that I was in a flaming hurry."

"Some hurry," she scoffed. "If you were really in a hurry," she added, nodding toward the snow, "you'd walk."

"That's an idea. But I left my snowshoes in the attic. Out! Go let Melly show you how to work the computer. You do realize that somebody's going to have to do her job while she's on her honeymoon?"

"Me? But, Cade, I don't know anything about computers. . . ."

"What a great time for you to learn," he advised. He searched her flushed face, seeing a new purpose in it, a slackening of the fear, and he nodded. "Don't rush off to New York after the wedding. Stay with me."

"I'd like to stay with you," she said in a soft, gentle tone as she looked into his dark eyes.

He held her gaze for a long, warm moment before he averted his eyes to the gearshift. "Now I'm going," he said firmly. "Either you skedaddle or you come with me."

"I'd like to come with you," she said with a sigh, "but I'd just get in the way, wouldn't I?"

"Sure," he said with a flash of white teeth. Then his eyes narrowed. "Do you want to come, really? Because I'm going to let you, and to hell with getting in the way, if you say yes."

She took a deep, slow breath, and shrugged. "Better not, I suppose," she said regretfully. "Melly's wedding dress . . . I have to get started."

"Okay. How about fabric?"

"Calla bought it for me; it's just a matter of deciding what to use," she told him. "Don't get sick, okay?"

He lifted an eyebrow. "Why? Afraid you'd have to nurse me?"

"I'd stay up all night for weeks if you needed me. Don't be silly," she chided, reaching for the door handle.

"Tell Calla not to keep supper, honey, it's going to be another long night."

She nodded as she held the door ajar. "Want me to bring your supper down to you?"

He smiled. "On your snowshoes? Better not, it's damned cold out here. I'll have a bite later. See you."

"See you."

She closed the door and watched him drive away with wistful eyes. She already regretted not going with him, but she didn't wait around to wonder why.

That night, she and Melly chose the fabric from the yards and yards of it that Calla had tucked away in the cedar chest.

"Isn't it strange that I'm getting married first?" Melly asked as they studied the pattern. "I always thought it would be you."

"Me and who?" Abby laughed.

"Cade, of course."

Abby caught her breath. "He never felt that way."

"Oh, you poor blind thing," Melly said softly. "He used to watch you like a man watching a rainbow. Sometimes his hands would tremble when he was helping you onto a horse or opening a door for you, and you never even noticed, did you?"

Abby's pale brown eyes widened helplessly. "Cade?"

"Cade." Melly sat back in her chair and sighed. "He was head over heels about you when you left here. He roared around for two weeks after you were gone, making the men nervous, driving the rest of us up walls. He'd sit by the fire at night and just stare straight ahead. I've never seen a man grieve like that over a woman. And you didn't even know."

Abby's eyes closed in pain. If she'd known that, career or no career, she would have come running back to Montana on her bare feet if she'd had to. "I didn't have any idea. If I'd known that, I never would have left here. Never!" she burst out.

Melly caught her breath at the passion that flared up in her sister's eyes. "You loved him?"

"Deathlessly." Her eyes closed, then opened again, misty with tears. "I'll die loving him."

"Abby!"

She took a steadying breath and slumped. "Four years. Four long years, and a nightmare at the end of it. And if I'd stayed here . . . why didn't he tell me?"

"I suppose he thought he was doing the best thing

for you," Melly said gently. "You were so excited about a career in modeling."

"I thought at the time that it would be better to moon over Cade at a distance instead of going to seed while I waited in vain for him to notice me again," Abby said miserably.

"Again?"

Darn Melly's quick mind. "Just never you mind. Let's go over this pattern."

"He still cares about you," Melly murmured.

"In a different way, though."

"That could change," came the soft reply, "if you want it to."

"If only Cade didn't have such a soft spot for stray things," Abby said, her eyes wistful. "I never know what he really feels—I never have. He was sorry for me when I was a kid and, in a way, he still is. I don't want a man who pities me, Melly."

"How do you know that Cade does? You're a lovely woman."

"A woman with a very big problem," Abby reminded her, "and Cade goes out of his way to help people, you know that. We go back a long way and he's fond of me. How can I be sure that what he feels isn't just compassion, Melly?"

"Give it time and find out."

"That," she said with a sigh, "is sage advice. By the way, you're going to have to teach me how to do your job, because he's already maneuvered me into replacing you while you're on your honeymoon."

"Oh, he has, has he?" Melly pursed her lips and her

eyes laughed. "That isn't something he'd do if he really felt sorry for you!" she assured her sister.

"Now cut that out! Here, tell me if you like the dress better with a long train or a short one. . . ."

And for the rest of the night, they concentrated on the wedding gown.

8

In the days that followed, Abby learned more about the logistics of roundup on Painted Ridge than she wanted to. The whole ranch suddenly revolved around preparations for it. There were supplies to get in, men to hire and add to the weekly payroll. And at the head of it all was Cade, mapping out strategy, tossing out orders as he organized everything from the butane for the torches they used to heat the branding irons to ear tags. At the same time, he was involved with roundup on the other two ranches he had interests in, and in between were cattle auctions, board meetings and a rushed trip to New York to discuss his corporation's plans to buy a feedlot in Oklahoma.

Abby couldn't help thinking how sexy Cade looked in his pale grey suit with matching boots and Stetson when he came downstairs with his suitcase in his hand.

"Well, I guess I'm ready," he grumbled, heading toward the front door. Hank was waiting impatiently outside in the truck.

"You really need something snazzier than a pickup truck to ride to the airport in," Abby remarked with a smile. "You look very sophisticated."

He glanced at her, his eyes clearly approving her jeans and pale T-shirt. "I'd rather be wearing what you've got on."

"You'd sure look funny in it," she murmured wickedly.

He chuckled softly. "I guess I would. Oh, damn, I hate these dressup things, and I hate to ride around the country on airplanes with other people at the controls."

"If you fly like you drive—" she began.

"Cut that out," he said darkly. He checked his watch. "Stay off the horses until I get back, too. I told Hank to make sure you do."

Her eyes flashed, and she drew herself up to her full height, lifting her shoulders proudly. "I'm not a child."

His gaze went pointedly to the high, firm thrust of her breasts and he smiled faintly. "No, ma'am, you sure aren't."

"Cade Alexander McLaren!" she gasped.

He chuckled at her red face. "Well, you can't blame a man for noticing things, honey."

"Hank's leaning on the horn," she murmured, glancing nervously toward the door.

"Let him lean on it. Or stand on it. Hank was born in a hurry." He studied her for a long moment. "I'll let you kiss me goodbye if you ask me nice."

She colored even more. "Why do I always have to do all the kissing?" she asked.

"Because you might not like the way I do it," he said.

"Are you sure?" Her heart pounded wildly and she felt her breath coming hard and fast when she saw the expression that washed over his dark face. He dropped the suitcase with a hard thud and strode right for her.

Before she even had time to decide whether to run or duck, he had her by the waist. He lifted her completely off the floor so that she was on a level with his glittering dark eyes, and she noticed that he was breathing as raggedly as she was.

"Let's see, Abby," he said quietly, and tilted his head.

His mouth bit softly at hers in brief, rough kisses that made her blood run hot. Her hands tangled in his dark hair as she tried to hold his mouth over hers, hungry to feel the full pressure of it. Her body felt taut as a cord and she opened her lips to the coaxing play of his. It seemed to be just what he was waiting for, because he took possession then, and she felt his tongue go into her mouth in an intimacy they'd shared only once before.

She caught a sharp breath, but she didn't protest. Not even when he eased her sensuously down and held her close against his taut body. He forced her mouth open further, tasting it with growing hunger, increasing the pressure until she moaned with sudden pleasure.

One big hand released her and slid up her side to

her breast. It hesitated for an instant, and then it engulfed her, his thumb coaxing a helpless response even through two layers of fabric. She moaned again.

He lifted his mouth, breathing roughly, and studied her rapt face. "Look, Abby," he whispered, glancing down to the darkness of his hand where her body was frankly showing its response to his touch. "See how you react to me. . . ."

"Don't," she whispered achingly, pushing his hand away even as she leaned her head against his vest while she caught her breath. Her heartbeat was still rapid, and she felt flushed with embarrassment.

His forehead nuzzled against her soft blond hair. "Don't be shy with me," he said quietly. "I know you wouldn't let another man touch you like this. I don't think less of you for it."

Tears welled in her eyes. He was the most tender man she'd ever known; he had a way of making the most traumatic things seem easy, uncomplicated.

"It shocked me a little," she whispered unsteadily.

"I like the way you kiss me when you're shocked," he mused with a faint smile when he lifted his head.

Her eyes darkened as she looked up at him, unafraid. "I tasted you," she whispered shakily.

His hands tautened like steel around her upper arms and his face seemed to harden even as she watched. "Don't say things like that to me," he said unsteadily. "You don't realize the effect it has, and I'm already late for the airport."

She looked down at his broad chest. "Sorry. Will you be gone long?"

His hands contracted and then released her. "A

couple days. I can't spare them, but I don't want the man to change his mind about that feedlot. The corporation needs it."

She nodded, glancing up at his set features. "I'll do my best not to foul up your bookkeeping while you're gone."

"Melly won't let you," he replied. He took a long breath and moved back to the suitcase, swinging it up easily. "Besides, all the bookkeeping we do here is payroll, and you'll be doing cattle records, not that. Take care, honey."

"You, too," she said softly, missing him already. He would take the color away when he left. It had been that way all her adult life.

Hank was blowing the horn again, and Cade shook his head. "He's afraid the plane will leave me behind," he said amusedly. "I chewed him out this morning for forgetting to put in a supply order. He feels safer when I'm a state or two away."

"Don't they all," she murmured with a wicked grin.

He tilted the Stetson low over his eyes. "Bye. Don't kiss any other boys while I'm gone, okay?"

"What's the matter, afraid I might make comparisons?" She laughed.

"How did you know?" He winked at her and walked down the steps without looking back, yelling at Hank to stop wearing out his best horn.

Abby spent her time with Melly, learning how to use the computer. It gave the sisters time to talk and get reacquainted, and it gave Abby something to occupy her mind.

Even when Cade returned, she hardly saw him. He was up with the dawn and out past dark, getting everything ready for the roundup and the massive task of moving the cattle up to summer pasture. By the end of the week, Abby could pick out a single registered bull from the herd records, print out the information required and do it without losing a single punctuation mark.

Meanwhile, Cade, in his spare time, dictated one letter after another to Melly and answered the flood of phone calls that never seemed to stop. The next week, Cade was called out from signing letters at his desk by one of the men when his prize-winning bull keeled over in the barn. He went stalking out the door with Abby at his heels. Melly and Jerry had gone out just after breakfast, and Abby was trying to keep up with Cade's machine-gun dictation and quick temper all alone.

Abby followed him outside with a typed letter in her hand as he took the reins of his black gelding from one of the men and started to swing into the saddle.

"Cade, could you sign this letter before you go?" she called. "It's about that new hay baler."

"Oh, hell, I forgot," he muttered. "Hand it here, honey."

He propped it against the saddle and slashed his name in a bold scrawl across the bottom of it. "I'll see if—"

"Mr. McLaren," one of the new cowboys interrupted, reining up beside them. "Hank said to find you and tell you that the new tractor we just bought is busted. Axle broke clean in half on us while we were planting over in the bottoms. Hank says you want we should call that feller who sold it to us and see if it's still under warranty? The other tractor's still down, you know. Billy's trying to fix it, and we loaned three out to Mr. Hastings and let Jones have one. . . ."

"Oh, good God," Cade muttered angrily. "All right, tell Hank to check with the salesman and see how long it will take to get a replacement."

"Yes, sir," the cowboy agreed politely. "And the hardware wants to know if you'll want any more butane."

Cade looked positively hunted. "They can wait until I get through looking at my sick bull, can't they?" he asked the man. "Damn it, son, that bull cost me a quarter of a million dollars, and the insurance won't heal my heart if he dies!" He glowered at the cowboy. "Tell Jerry to take care of it."

"Uh, he's kind of busy," the young cowboy muttered, avoiding Cade's eyes.

"Doing what?" came the terse reply.

"Uh, he and Miss Melly are down at their house, her house, checking paint swatches . . ."

Cade's cheeks colored darkly with temper. "You get down there and tell Jerry I said he can stop that kind of thing. I pay him to run this damned ranch, not to go around checking paint swatches on my time!"

"Yes, sir, Mr. McLaren!" He saluted and rode quickly away.

Abby was watching Cade with twinkling eyes. It was something else to watch him delegate. He did it well, and his temper mostly amused the men because it was never malicious.

He turned, catching that gleam in her eyes, and cocked an eyebrow at her from under the wide-brimmed hat. "Something tickle your fancy, Miss Shane?"

"You," she admitted quietly. "I just stand in awe of you, Mr. McLaren."

He chuckled softly. "And you thought a rancher's life was all petting cattle, I suppose?"

"I grew up here," she reminded him. "But I never realized just how much work it was until I started helping Melly. How do you stand it, Cade?"

"I'm used to it." He was holding the reins in one hand, but he reached out and drew his fingers down her cheek. "I love it. The way you love the glitter of your own work, I imagine, miss model."

"I wish you wouldn't make fun of what I do," she said sadly, searching his dark eyes. "I've worked very hard to get where I am. And modeling is much more than painting on a pretty face and smiling."

He withdrew his hand and lit a cigarette. "It must seem pretty tame to you out here."

"Tame?" Her eyes widened. "Are you kidding?"

He frowned thoughtfully, and his searching eyes caught hers. They stared at each other quietly, while the silence grew tense and electric around them, and her lips parted under a wild rush of breath.

His breath was coming hard, too. He dropped the reins as if he couldn't help himself and moved close, so that she could feel the heat of his body and the smell the spicy cologne that clung to him. Her eyes went to his mouth and she wanted it so much that she ached with the wanting.

His steely fingers bit into her waist. "Want to kiss me, Abby Shane?" he asked roughly.

"Very much," she whispered, unembarrassed and unintimidated as she looked into his darkening eyes. "Lift me up, please. . . ."

She felt his hands contract, and she seemed to float within reach of that chiseled mouth. Her hands slid around his neck to the back of his head and she eased her mouth onto his, letting her lips part softly as they touched him.

His head tilted and his mouth opened under hers with a heavy sigh. He didn't insist, but she could sense his own growing hunger, and she fed it. Her lips nibbled softly at his, her tongue eased out to trace the firm line of his upper lip. And the reaction she got was startling.

All at once, she was swept against the long, hard line of his body and he was kissing her, violently. His mouth demanded in a kiss so sensuous she moaned at the sensations it aroused. She felt his tongue in her mouth, against her lips. A shudder worked its way down her body and fires blazed up in her blood.

"No," she protested when he tried to lift his dark head. She trembled in his arms as she clung. "Cade, please, just once more. . . ."

She heard the ragged breath he took before his mouth crushed back against hers, warm and rough and forceful for an instant. Then she was back on her feet again and leaning heavily against him, his lips brushing her forehead.

"What do you want from me, Abby?" he ground out.

Your love, she thought miserably. I want you to love me as fiercely as I love you. "I'm sorry," she muttered against his shirt front. "I like kissing you."

He was trying to get his breath back, or at least it sounded that way. "I like kissing you, too. But I'm a man, not a boy. Kissing isn't enough for me anymore."

Her fingers curled against his shirt, and she could feel the thick hair on his chest through it. She wanted to open his shirt and touch him there. Involuntarily, her fingers moved across his chest and he shuddered.

"No, baby," he said softly. He stilled her hands, and she wondered dizzily what had happened to the cigarette he'd been holding. Her eyes found it, smoking away in the dirt, where he must have flung it.

She sighed wearily, loving the comforting feel of his hands at her back. She didn't want to move away from him, but it was obvious that he wasn't going to let her get any closer.

"I forgot," she murmured.

"What?"

She drew away and grinned, although her heart was aching. "That you're wary of us wild city girls," she said, her light brown eyes sparkling in the pale frame of her hair. "You needn't worry, Cade, I'm not quite strong enough to wrestle you down in a haystack."

Her quip should have made him smile, but it didn't. He searched her face for a long time, touching every curve and line of it with his eyes. "I think we both need to remember that you're here to recuperate, Abby," he said after a minute. "This is temporary.

You've got a successful career waiting for you in New York, but this is my world." He nodded toward the distant hills, dotted with red-coated, white-faced Herefords. "I don't have time for casual flings, even if I believed in them."

She drew away from him as if she'd been burned. "Excuse me for throwing myself at you. . . ."

"Stop it." His fingers caught her upper arms and held her in front of him when she would have moved away. "A few kisses aren't going to hurt either of us. I just want you to understand the limits. You're very vulnerable right now, Abby. You could easily make a decision that you'd regret for the rest of your life."

He was speaking in riddles, and she stared up at him with wounded eyes, because it sounded as if he were gently rejecting her. Well, she should be used to it, shouldn't she? And if he could be adult about it, so could she. Damn her breaking heart, she'd never let him see it!

Keep it light, girl, she told herself, keep your pride, at least. She managed a bright smile. "Sensible Cade," she murmured. "Don't worry, I promise not to rip your clothes off."

He tried to smother a chuckle and failed. "That would be one for the books, in several ways." He touched her lips with a lazy finger. "Abby, I've never undressed in front of a woman."

She could feel her own surprise coloring her cheeks. "Never?" she burst out.

"Look who's shocked," he mused. "Have you ever stripped for a man?"

"For you, once," she reminded him, avoiding his

suddenly explosive gaze. "It was an accident, of course, I had no idea you were anywhere near the ranch that night."

"I know that." A rough sound broke from his throat, as if an unwanted memory was plaguing him. "I'd better go see about that bull. We'll be moving cattle into the pens today. If that call I'm expecting from California comes, take the number and call Hank on the radio. He'll find me."

"Yes, boss," she said smartly.

He looked down at her with narrowed eyes. "How did you get so short?"

"I'm wearing flat-heeled shoes," she said. "And you tower over everybody."

He grinned. "Keeps the men intimidated."

"Your temper's enough to do that." She laughed. "Don't work yourself into a stupor."

"Work keeps my mind off other things," he returned, letting his eyes run boldly up and down her body. "If it's pretty tomorrow, I'll take you on a picnic."

Her whole face brightened and she smiled so sweetly that his eyes froze on her and couldn't seem to move away.

"Down by the river?" she asked hopefully.

"You love those damned cottonwoods and pines, don't you?" he asked.

"It's spring," she reminded him. "I love the color of the cottonwoods when they're just budding out. The softest kind of green, and the grass is just beginning to get lush. . . ."

"Well, I need to check the fences down there," he mused.

"You work all the time," she grumbled. "You can't even go on a picnic without combining it with business!"

"The ranch isn't my business, Abby. It's my life," he said quietly.

She sighed angrily. "Don't I know it? You're married to it!"

His dark eyes narrowed. "What else have I got?" he demanded.

The question startled her. She watched him swing gracefully into the saddle. The rich leather creaked under his formidable weight as he settled himself and gripped the reins.

"Don't forget about that California call," he said. "And keep close to the house. I don't know some of these new men except by reputation."

"Cowboys are mostly polite and courteous," she reminded him.

"And some of them aren't." He stared down at her hard. "I'd kill a man who tried to hurt you while you were on my land. You keep that in mind."

He wheeled the big horse and went cantering away, leaving Abby standing in the shade of the trees, staring after him. She hadn't needed to ask if he meant that threat. She knew him too well. In the old days, when he was younger and much more hot-tempered, she'd seen him give "object lessons" to cowboys who thought they could push him. He was quick on his feet, and he knew how to handle himself in a fight. The men might grin when he blustered around in a temper over ranch problems, but they knew just the same that there was a line nobody crossed with him.

She wrapped her arms around herself and walked

back into the house. It was only then that she realized how vague the memory of the attack was becoming. Being here, away from the city, had given her new perspective, healed the mental wounds. She'd be more careful in the future, but she wouldn't let that one bad experience ruin her life. Her mind kept going back to what Cade had said, about giving the would-be rapist rights over her. Trust him to know the right thing to say.

She wandered back into the den and sat down at the computer. She was glad Cade didn't have a ranch office as such, like many cattlemen did. The den was comfortable and informal, and she liked its homey atmosphere.

The sudden jangling of the phone made her jump, but she recovered quickly and reached for it.

"McLaren Ranch office," she said automatically.

"Abby Shane, please," came a pleasant female voice in reply.

"This is she."

There was a tinkling laugh. "Well, I've run you down at last. This is Jessica Dane, Abby. Has Melly mentioned me to you?"

The boutique owner! Abby's pale brown eyes glittered with excitement. "Heavens, yes!" she returned, bubbling over. "I was afraid she'd got it wrong and you weren't really interested."

"I was, I am, but I couldn't catch you in your apartment." Jessica laughed. "Now I've got you trapped. Listen, I own a little boutique over the border from you in Sheridan, Wyoming. I'm never going to be able to compete with Saks, you understand, but I have a good mail order business in addition to a thriving shop."

"Yes, I've heard all about your success from Melly," Abby said. "She thinks you carry the prettiest leisure clothes short of New York."

"And that's why I'm bothering you," the other woman replied. "Those dresses you designed for Melly are just what I'm looking for to add to my spring and summer line. They're simple and elegant, they wouldn't cost a fortune to make and my customers would eat them up."

"Do you mean it?" Abby burst out.

"Of course I mean it. We could work something out, if you're interested. I know you make a lot modeling—I broke out of that rat race ten years ago and risked everything to open this shop. Now I'm making just as much as I did in New York, but my feet don't hurt so much anymore," she added with laughter in her voice.

"You were a model? Then you know how it is, don't you?" she asked.

Jessica laughed. "Oh, yes, I know very well. I spent half my time trying to stay out of trouble, and I imagine it's even worse now."

"I don't just go to the parties," Abby confessed, "and I keep to myself. But then, too, I'm not in that top ten percent. Frankly, I'm sick of it all. I can't think of anything I love more than designing. . . ."

"Then why not do some work for me?" Jessica pleaded. "At least think about it. I know we could come to an arrangement. You could come down here and look over my business, and I could show you what I have in mind."

"I'd like that," Abby said. "I have commitments lined up for the next few months, but come late September, I'm a free agent. Could I let you know then?"

"Fine! Meanwhile, give me your address in New York and I'll send you some of my catalogs." There was a smile in the woman's voice. "Maybe they'll tempt you."

"I'm already tempted." Abby sighed.

"Good. You'll be easy to convince." She laughed. "Here, take down my number and call me the minute you make up your mind." She dictated the digits while Abby jotted them on her calendar. "By the way, Abby, are you going to be at Melly's wedding?"

"Yes. I designed her wedding dress."

"Fantastic! I'm invited, too, so we'll get a chance to meet then. We'll go off in a corner and I'll describe some of the new designs I'm looking for. How about that?"

"I can hardly wait," Abby said genuinely. "Jessica, I can't tell you how much I appreciate the offer."

"I'm the one who ought to do the thanking. You've got great potential, honey. And believe me, in the long run, you'll make as much designing for the boutique as you will trudging all over New York. And you can do it at your own pace, too."

"I hope I'm not dreaming all this. Thanks again, Jessica. I'll look forward to seeing you at the wedding."

"Me, too, honey. Have a nice day. Enjoyed it!"

"So did I!" Abby laughed. She hung up and stared

at the receiver in astonishment. It was like the answer to a prayer. She could give up the long hours and the stress and do what she loved best. She could even come home to Montana!

For one insane moment, she thought about going out to find Cade, to tell him. Maybe it would show him that she wanted to give up all the glitter he thought she couldn't do without. But as soon as the thought came, she shut it out. He'd just blow up if she interrupted him. And why should he care if she came home? He was letting her stay on his ranch to be near Melly and get herself back together. He might want her—why not?—she was an attractive woman. But wanting wasn't loving, and he was the world's most determined bachelor. Marriage wasn't in his vocabulary—he'd said as much. The ranch was his woman.

Abby sighed and pulled out the herd records she was working on. Anyway, it was nice to have a choice. She could look forward to talking to Jessica about her boutique, and it would pass the time.

The day was a long one, even after Melly came back to help her catch up with the work.

"I'm just tickled pink about Jessica's offer," Melly confided as she watched Abby seal a letter. "Are you going to do it?"

"I don't know," Abby said honestly. "I'd love to come home. But I don't know if I could bear it."

"The loneliness, you mean?"

"Being so close to Cade and so far away from him, all at once," Abby replied. Her eyes showed the wound of loving hopelessly. "I'd rather be hundreds of miles away than practically next door, Melly. If I can't have him, I'd just as soon not have to see him at all. It hurts too much."

"For someone who doesn't care, he sure kisses you a lot lately."

"He said it wouldn't hurt either one of us," she said bitterly. "But he reminded me all the same that I'm here to get over the attack, and I've got a career to go back to. You'd think he couldn't wait to get me off the place."

"Has it ever occurred to you that he might want you gone for the same reason you're going?" Melly asked quietly. "I get the idea that he doesn't think you could give up modeling."

"It's not that at all," Abby protested. "This ranch is his whole life. He's always talking about how stupid people are to get married, and that he never will. And almost in the same breath, he'll swear that he doesn't believe in affairs. I don't know what to make of him."

Melly threw up her hands. "I give up. You're as dense as he is. Okay, show me these records and I'll help you catch up. When are you supposed to get back to Jessica, by the way?"

"She's coming to the wedding, and we're going to talk. What does she look like?"

Melly grinned. "Wait and see. It'll be a revelation to you. Now, this is where we need to start taking off cattle. . . ."

They worked steadily until supper. Melly went out with Jerry to a friend's house. Abby had just finished changing her clothes and was telling a persistent caller for the fourth time in as many hours that Cade was still out when he came slamming angrily in the door. His face was rigid, his lips compressed. He was still wearing his chaps and the brim of his wide hat was crushed in one hand.

"Well, don't just stand there, for God's sake, hang that thing up and get the liniment," he muttered, hobbling up the stairs to his room.

"What happened?" she called after him, absently hanging up on the caller before she thought.

"Cow fell on me," he growled. "Hurry up, damn it!" He went into his bedroom and slammed the door.

Abby rushed into the kitchen to get the liniment. Calla got it out of the cabinet for her.

"Bull again, huh?" old Jeb asked from the doorway as he entered the kitchen.

"He said it was a cow," Abby volunteered.

"Told him he ought to let the younger boys wrestle them things." Jeb nodded. "Yep, I told him, but he wouldn't listen. He's got more broke bones and scars than any man I ever knowed. Lot of them were from his rodeo days, but he's got more being bull-headed and doing jobs he's too brittle for."

"He never listens," Calla agreed, nodding her head. "Why I remember one time . . ."

She was still going strong when Abby left the two of them recalling other incidents of Cade's intentional deafness.

He had his shirt off when she went into the bedroom. She closed the door behind her, hesitating. The last time she'd been in this particular room was that night when he'd carried her in from the swimming pool in nothing but her damp jeans. It brought back bittersweet memories.

"Open the door if you're nervous being alone with me," he growled, rubbing his shoulder.

"Sorry," she murmured, trying not to appear too interested in his naked chest. Without his shirt, he was the sexiest thing she'd ever seen, bronzed and muscular, with a thick wedge of dark, curling hair arrowing down to his flat stomach.

She uncapped the bottle of liniment and wrinkled her nose. "My gosh, you'd better make your men sign affidavits that they won't quit if I put this stuff on you."

"Shut up and rub," he grumbled, indicating the smooth flesh of his shoulder.

She poured liniment in her palm and began to apply it. Her fingers tingled at the feel of his flesh under them. "How did a cow manage to fall on you?"

"It's a long story." He lit a cigarette while she massaged the aching limb, wincing as she went over a tender spot.

"Should you smoke?" she murmured. "We might both blow up if a spark ignites the fumes. . . ."

He glared at her. His hair was tousled over his broad forehead, over his dark, glittering eyes and heavy brows, and he looked impossibly masculine.

"Funny girl," he mocked.

"Laughing beats crying, my papa always used to say," she reminded him.

He turned his eyes away and sighed. "I can't imagine you crying over me."

Abby blinked, wondering at how stupid God had made some men. "That works both ways. I'll bet you're just counting the days until I'm on my way back to New York."

He didn't answer her. He took a long draw from the cigarette and exhaled through pursed lips. "Nightmares fading away, honey?" he asked.

She managed a faint smile. "All but gone, in fact." She shrugged, applying more liniment. "It was so hellish at the time. But looking back, I was lucky. Really lucky. All he did was push me around a little before the bystanders chased him off. It was the idea of what could have happened that was so scary. Gosh, men are strong, Cade."

"Some men," he agreed. He glanced at her.

She looked down as he looked up, and her eyes drowned in his dark, intense stare. Her hands stilled on his arm, and time seemed to go into a standstill around them. She was remembering another night, another time, when she'd lain on this very bed in his arms and experienced her first intimacy with a man. But Cade had changed since then. The easygoing, humorous man she'd once known had been replaced by a far more mature man, a harder man. He'd never been easy to read, but now nothing showed in his expression.

He reached out without warning and caught her around the waist, pulling her down on the bed beside him.

"Cade!" she gasped, too shocked to struggle.

He rolled over on his side and one bare arm arched across her body to hold her there while he leaned on an elbow and watched the expressions cross her face. Her eyes dropped to his chest, and she wanted to touch him so desperately that she closed them to resist the impulse.

"Afraid?" he asked softly.

Her fingers touched his hard face, sensitive to the rough texture of it where he needed a shave, to the feel of his cool, thick hair against them. "I'm with you now. I'm safe."

"Not so safe," he said with a faint smile. "But protected, for what it's worth. Suppose I kiss you half to death and then I can grab a bite to eat and go back out."

"Suppose you just kiss me half to death and forget about going back out?" she asked, tingling all over as she waited to feel that hard, warm mouth over hers.

"Because," he breathed, fitting his lips slowly, sensitively to hers, "as sure as God made little green apples, Calla's going to be knocking at that door any minute to make sure you're safe. And once I'm fed, she'll want to make sure that I'm too tired to find my way to you."

"Calla wouldn't . . ."

He kissed her slowly, softly. "Calla would. She's not blind. She sees the way I look at you."

Her heart was racing. "How do you look at me?" she asked.

His mouth smiled mockingly against hers. "Haven't

you noticed? Hush. I seem to have waited half my life to get you in bed with me like this. . . ."

She felt his lips nibbling at hers, nudging at them with exquisite slowness, and she relaxed, letting her fingers curl into the hair at his nape.

His tongue teased its way into her mouth and she gasped sharply at the sudden intimacy, even as she felt his body moving sensuously against hers. His mouth softened and became coaxing with expert sureness as his chest scraped abrasively, teasingly across her breasts until the tips hardened. She moaned softly and he lifted his dark head to look into her eyes, searching them quickly. "Was that fear or pleasure?" he whispered.

Her lips parted involuntarily. One slender hand moved from the back of his head down over his chest and stroked him, smoothing the curling dark hair over the warm muscles. "I'm not afraid of you," she said in a breathless whisper, searching his dark eyes.

"I could make you afraid, though, couldn't I, Abby?" he asked, as if it mattered. "You're still very vulnerable."

"You make me sound like a terrified virgin," she replied.

His warm fingers stroked the long, pale hair back from her flushed face. "I'm doing my damndest to remember that you are one," he said softly. "It's hard for a man to make love like this, Abby. To remember not to kiss too hard, not to touch too intimately. . . ."

Her eyes betrayed the surprise she felt at what he was confessing. "Have you been deliberately holding back all this time?" she asked, searching his eyes. "Because you thought you might frighten me?"

He drew in a deep breath, and she felt his chest expand against her breasts. "I couldn't bear to hurt you," he said. His voice was like velvet, deep and dark and softly textured. "I've treated you like porcelain since you've been here. I've damned near worked myself into an early grave to keep away . . . and tonight, I caved in. I kept remembering how you were this morning, how you begged for my mouth. . . ." His eyes closed, his face tautened. "Oh, God, Abby, what am I going to do about you?" he groaned.

She couldn't even speak. He looked so incredibly vulnerable, as if he were at the end of some imaginary rope. Her fingers stroked his broad shoulders, loving the very texture of his skin. She loved everything about him, every line and curve of him.

"You said this morning," she reminded him softly, "that a few kisses wouldn't hurt either one of us. Didn't you?"

His eyes opened, and they were like black fires. "And that's the whole problem, little one. I want more than a few kisses."

Her eyes fell to his chiseled mouth and she felt her body begin to tremble. "Cade . . . I don't mind if you touch me," she whispered.

His face moved against hers, his breath sighing out heavily at her ear. "That could be dangerous."

With a surge of fearlessness, she caught one of the

Coming Next Month

Fancy Free by Suzanne Michelle

Terri King had set aside everything to establish her charter service—including men. Then she met movie star Ryder Jack and found herself soaring to heights she never dreamed possible.

This Wildfire Magic by Sara Chance

Desiree Beaumont literally dreamed up her ideas. When she met Zackery Taylor, the man who had purchased exclusive rights to her line of lingerie, she realised he was her dream come true.

Ballinger's Rule by Eve Gladstone

Caitlin fought Keith Ballinger in order to renovate Glenkiddy, an ancient Irish estate, with all her Irish wit and elfin magic. Then she realized that nothing but love would bend Ballinger's rule.

hands beside her on the bed and lifted it in hers. Before her courage gave out completely, she took it to her T-shirt and eased it hesitantly over the soft curve of her breast.

She wasn't prepared for the sensations it caused. She drew in a sharp breath and bit her lip to keep from crying out.

Cade lifted his dark head and looked at her, holding her eyes while his hand pressed softly against her. His thumb moved onto the taut peak and teased it. His heart slammed wildly against her with the action, and she could see the desire that was smoldering in his eyes.

"Four years," he said in a hunted tone. "And I haven't forgotten a second of it. I remember the way you looked, the way you cried out when I touched you like this."

"Do you think I don't remember, too?" she asked under her breath. "I lived on it for years, Cade—" Her voice broke, her mouth trembled as she looked up at him.

"So did I," he breathed out shakily. He bent again and let his mouth brush warmly against her parted lips. "You were so young. You still are. Years too young, and a world away from me. Abby, are you wearing anything under this?"

She wished she were more sophisticated. She blushed, feeling her body stiffen as he slid his hand under the hem of the shirt and up to find the answer himself. He caught his breath when he touched her, really touched her, and felt the helpless response of her soft, bare flesh.

Her own hands reached up to stroke the tangled mat of hair on his chest. "I used to dream about touching you like this," she confessed, watching him. "Feeling you . . ."

"Oh, God!" he ground out, trembling. His free hand cupped her head and held it still while his mouth devoured hers in the static stillness of the room. She felt his other hand moving over her bareness in a long, aching caress that made her arch up and moan with exquisite pleasure.

She protested once, gently, drawing away to breathe.

"Come back here," he murmured, "I'm not through."

"I have to breathe," she whispered as he turned her mouth back to his.

"Breathe me," he murmured against her soft, eager mouth. His hands smoothed over her back, pushing up the shirt as they swept with warm abrasiveness across her soft skin.

"You told me once that you'd never let another man touch you this way. Did you mean it?" he asked roughly.

"I meant it," she whispered, her voice trembling. Her fingers were clinging at the nape of his neck, her body arching to give him freer access to it. "I've never, ever wanted a man . . . after you."

Breathing like a distance runner, he lifted his head and looked down at her where the shirt was pulled up. His eyes darkened with a hunger she could actually see. Against her pale golden flesh, his hands were as dark as leather.

"You can't imagine how it feels," she breathed, her eyes loving him.

"Being touched?" he asked, lifting his eyes to watch her rapt face.

She shook her head slowly. "Being with you . . . like this. Oh, Cade, I'd be embarrassed with my own sister, but I love it when you look at me . . . this way."

His breathing, already ragged, seemed to freeze inside him. His thumbs edged up, dragging softly against the rigid peaks, and she moaned sharply, looking straight into his eyes.

All at once he removed his hands and sat up, his big body shuddering with the force of his heartbeat, his eyes reckless and faintly dangerous.

"That's enough," he said roughly.

But it wasn't for Abby, and without even thinking, she followed him, kneeling just in front of him. She placed her trembling hands on his shoulders and swayed close, brushing her body softly, slowly against his hair-roughened chest, watching her own paleness disappearing into the curling hair with awe.

"Abby," he whispered shakily. His hands moved to her bare back and brought her slowly against him, prolonging the contact, easing her closer with a rhythm that made her tremble all the way to her toes.

His hands caught her hips and ground them against his, and she cried out as she felt the force of his hunger. Trembling, her arms locked around his neck as they fell sideways on the bed. He was beside her,

then they shifted, and she felt his full weight evenly distributed along the length of her aching body. She could feel the abrasiveness of his wiry hair against her bareness where they touched, the scent of the liniment becoming as potent as perfume as they kissed wildly, and she wondered at the depth of her own love for him.

Feeling unusually reckless, she began to move. Her hands slid down his back to the base of his spine, and the mouth crushing hers groaned harshly. Against her body, he was warm and hard and she could feel every steely muscle in him. Even all those years ago, it had never been like this between them. The feel of him drowned her in sensation, in need and half-awakened hunger. She wanted to be closer than this, she wanted all the fabric out of the way, she wanted his eyes and his hands to touch her. She shifted restlessly, hungry as she never had been in her life, needing him . . . !

She touched him with hands that trembled, delighting in the feel of his smooth back muscles. Her fingers moved around to caress the thick mat of hair over his chest, and hesitantly, softly, traced the arrow of hair that ran below his belt. I love you, she thought silently. I love you. . . .

Cade's big body contracted as if he'd been shot, and all at once he seemed to come to his senses. He muttered a harsh curse and jerked himself away from Abby, rolling over to lie on his back. His body shuddered with frustrated need; his eyes closed, his jaw tautened. His breath came wildly. Watching him, she felt guilty that she'd let it go so far, because they'd

both known all the time that Cade wasn't going over his own limits. Only she'd forgotten, and he hadn't.

Fumbling, she pulled down her blouse with shaking hands and sat up. She took a deep breath and threw her legs over the side of the bed. "Excuse me," she said in a barely audible voice, "I didn't know where the limits were."

"Well, you found out, didn't you?" he shot at her.

She got off the bed and glanced toward him. He was pale, and his face was drawn as he sat up and reached for his shirt.

"I'm sorry," she said unsteadily. "I . . . I know it's unpleasant for men to . . . well . . ."

"Don't turn the knife," he said. His voice was cutting. He dragged a cigarette from his pocket and lit it with unsteady hands. "Damn it, Abby, I can't handle it when you do unexpected things like that! You knocked me right off balance."

She tried to smile. "And after I promised not to try and have my way with you, too."

But he didn't smile. His face grew harder. "You're tearing me inside out," he said, standing. "If I'd thought I could stand Calla's infernal sarcasm, I would have let her put the liniment on!"

"Next time I'll remember that," she shot back. She whirled, her eyes simmering with anger. "You started it!" she accused childishly.

His nostrils flared. "Yes, I started it," he said under his breath. "Nothing's changed. Nothing! I touch you, and we both start trembling. It was that way when you were only eighteen, and I carried you in here, wanting

you until I was just about out of my mind!" He ran an angry hand through his thick hair and glared up at her. "But I didn't take you then, and I won't take you now. There's no future in it. There never was."

"What an ego," she threw back. "My God, you're full of yourself!"

"That's what you think," he said harshly. "I went through the motions of work all day, but all I could think about was how it felt when we kissed this morning. I remembered your mouth the way a man dying of thirst remembers ice water, soft and sweet. Just how much do you think I can take?"

"Well, don't strain yourself," she said, turning away with a hot ache all the way to her toes. "I'll be gone soon enough."

"I know that," he said. His voice sounded hollow. The mattress creaked as he got to his feet. "Sex is a lousy foundation for a relationship, Abby. We're not going to build on it."

She flushed in spite of herself, but she wouldn't turn and let him see it. "Amen," she agreed. "If you want to call off the picnic tomorrow—"

"No," he said unexpectedly. "No, I don't want to call it off. It will be the last time we have together."

He said that as if it meant forever—that they'd never spend another minute alone—and she wanted to scream and cry and beg him to try and love her just a little. But she clenched her jaw and drew in a steadying breath. "Calla's going to scream about fixing a picnic with those new hands to feed."

"We'll risk it," he said shortly. "Right now, I've got to get back to the barn. That damned bull's improving

a little, but I want to see what the vet has to say when he checks him for the night."

"I could pack you a sandwich and some coffee," she offered.

"I don't want anything."

She opened the door and paused. "Especially me?" She laughed shakily and ran down the stairs with tears shimmering in her eyes.

9

Calla was cursing a blue streak when Abby walked into the kitchen the next morning at six, wearing a yellow sundress with an elasticized bodice and tiny straps that tied over each shoulder.

"Having to fry bacon and chicken all at once," the housekeeper muttered darkly as she stood over the stove. "Picnics, with all I got to do!" She glared over her shoulder at Abby. "Well, don't just stand there, girl, go set the table!"

"Yes, ma'am," Abby said smartly and curtsied. The dress was one she'd designed herself, and with her loosened blond hair, she looked like something out of a fashion magazine. Calla stopped muttering long enough to give her an approving stare. "Nice," she said after a minute. "You make that yourself?"

"Sure did." She whirled around for Calla's benefit, her skirt flying against her long, smooth legs. "It's cool

and comfortable and it doesn't bind. I'll make you one, if you like."

"I can just see me in something like that." The older woman sighed, indicating the dowdy housedress that covered her ample figure. Then her watery blue eyes narrowed. "You watch Cade while you're out there alone with him, you hear me? I ain't blind. I saw how you looked when you came out of his room last night. You make him keep his distance."

Abby felt her cheeks go hot. "Now, Calla . . ."

"Don't you 'now, Calla' me! I know Cade. He hasn't been the same since you walked through the front door, and it ain't because of the cattle." Her chin lifted. "You and I both know how he feels about weddings, Abigail," she added gently, using the younger woman's full name, as she rarely did except when she was serious. "You're my lamb, and I love him, too, but I don't want you hurt. Melly told me what happened. Don't you jump out of the frying pan into the fire. All you'll find here is heartache."

Abby smothered an urge to hug the concerned old woman, knowing it wouldn't be welcome. "You're sure about that?" she asked softly.

"He looks at you like a starving man looks at a steak smothered with onions," Calla replied. "But once he's fed, young lady, he's just as likely to find he's lost his taste for steak. You get my meaning? Wanting ain't loving."

"I know that," she said on a wistful sigh.

"Then act accordingly. He's been sticking close to the ranch for quite a while now," Calla added gently. "A hungry man is dangerous."

"I'm a big girl," Abby reminded her. "I can look out for myself—most of the time, anyway."

"And what time you can't, I will," came the fervent promise. "Now go set the table."

"Yes, ma'am," Abby said, grinning.

She carried two place settings of everyday china into the dining room and helped put the food on the table. Cade was uncharacteristically late getting downstairs, and she was almost ready to go up and call him when he walked into the room.

He looked as if he hadn't slept a wink. His dark hair was damp from a shower, and he was wearing a tan patterned Western shirt over rust-colored denims, and polished tan boots. He looked rugged and formidable, and so solemn that he intimidated her.

"I thought you were going to fix fences," Abby remarked.

"I am," he muttered. He sat down at the head of the table and stared at her for a long moment, taking in every line of her face and body. "When you finish your breakfast, go back upstairs and get dressed. I'm not taking you on a picnic half-naked."

The sudden attack left her dumb. She gaped at him with wide, hurt eyes before she put down her napkin and got up from the table in tears. She'd worn the sundress especially for him, to please him.

"Where you going?" Calla demanded, elbowing in with a platter of scrambled eggs.

"To put on some clothes," Abby said in a subdued tone, and didn't look back.

"Now what have you done?" Calla was demanding, but Abby didn't wait around to hear the answer.

She rushed up to her room and slammed the door with tears boiling down her flushed cheeks.

She cried for what seemed hours before she dragged herself up and put on her blue jeans and a short-sleeved blue blouse. She put on a vest over that, a fringed leather one, and put her hair up in a bun. Before she went back downstairs, she scrubbed off every trace of makeup as well.

When she walked back into the room, pale and silent, Cade barely glanced at her.

"If you'd like to call the picnic off, I can finish Melly's wedding dress instead," she said as she sipped her coffee, ignoring the eggs and sausage and fresh, hot biscuits.

"I'd like to call everything off, if you want to know," he said shortly.

"That's fine with me. I have plenty to keep me busy." She finished her coffee and, trying not to let him see how hurt she really was, smiled in his general direction and got up.

"Abby."

She stopped, keeping her back to him. "What?"

He drew in a slow breath. "Let's talk."

"I can't think what we have to talk about," she said with a careless laugh, turning to face him with fearless eyes. "I'll be leaving as soon as Melly comes back after her honeymoon, you know. But I can go right now, if you like. I've had an interesting offer from a boutique owner—"

His eyes flashed fire, and he cut her off sharply before she could tell him the rest. "And you'll be off to another landmark in your career, I suppose?" he

asked with a mocking smile. "It's just as well, honey; I plan to do some traveling of my own in the next few months. There's only one job here, and Melly's got it."

"Don't worry, I don't particularly enjoy keeping records on cattle," she replied with a cool smile.

He stood up and lit a cigarette, leaving his second cup of coffee untouched on the table. "Calla's got the picnic basket packed. We might as well spend today together. It'll sure as hell be the last time we have, because starting tomorrow I'll be out with the boys constantly."

"Why don't you take Calla on a picnic?" she asked coldly. "You like her."

His nostrils flared as he stared down at her from his superior height. "I used to like you pretty well," he reminded her.

"Sure, as long as I stayed away." She moved about restlessly. "I should have stayed in New York. I didn't think I'd be welcomed here with open arms. . . ."

"You might have been, once," he said enigmatically, "if you hadn't decided that the world of fashion meant more to you than a home and family."

She glanced up at him narrowly. "Pull the other one." She laughed. "If I'd stayed here, I would have withered away and become just another old maid dotting the landscape, and you know it. Or are you going to try and tell me that you were dying for love of me?" she added mockingly.

His dark eyes went quietly over her face. "Why would I waste time telling you something you wouldn't believe in the first place?" he asked. "If we're going, let's go. I don't have time to stand around talking."

"Oh, by all means, the ranch might fall apart!" she replied, and walked into the kitchen.

Calla glanced at her and scowled, a scowl that grew even fiercer when she saw Cade. "There's the basket," she grumbled at him.

"Thanks a hell of a lot," Cade snapped back, grabbing the picnic basket. "If you need extra help here, hire it. Or quit. But don't bother me with it. I'm slam out of patience, Calla."

And he slammed his hat over his brow and stormed out the back door ahead of Abby.

"Watch out," the housekeeper said sympathetically. "Something's eating him today."

"If he keeps that up, I'll find something that really will eat him!" Abby promised. "A wandering cannibal . . ." she muttered as she followed him out the door.

Cade drove them through pastures where there were little more than ruts for the truck to follow, and Abby held onto the seat for dear life, afraid to say a word. His face was grim, eyes doggedly on the ruts, and he looked as if the slightest sound would set him off.

But later, after he'd stripped off his shirt and rewired two or three strands of barbed wire in a pasture near the river, he seemed to have worked off some of his irritation.

Abby, who'd already spread out the picnic lunch under the cottonwoods near the river, wandered through the towering break of pines and spruce to find him.

He was leaning back against the truck smoking a

cigarette, his eyes on the distant mountains across the rolling grasslands. His hat was off, his gloves were still in place and he looked as much a part of the land as the tall grasses that grew there. With his shirt gone, his chest was revealed, the thick wedge of hair damp with sweat, his tanned shoulders gleaming with moisture. Abby almost closed her eyes at the sight of all that provocative masculinity so close and tempting. She wanted desperately to touch him, to run her hands over those broad shoulders and feel the texture of the thick hair that covered the bronzed muscles of his chest. But she didn't dare.

"Lunch is ready, when you are," she said quietly.

He glanced at her solemnly. "I've patched the fence," he said. His eyes went back to the mountains. "God, I love this country," he added in a tone deep and soft with reverence. "I could stand and look over it for hours and never tire of the sight."

"It wouldn't have been much different in the old days, when trappers and fur traders and explorers like William Clark came here," she remarked, going to stand beside him. The wind was tearing at the tight bun of her hair, but she pinned it back relentlessly.

"It's different," Cade said shortly, his eyes straight ahead. "It's damned hard balancing between environmental protection and progress, Abby."

"Between mining and ranching, agriculture and industry?" she asked gently, because it was a subject that could set him off like a time bomb.

"Exactly." He glanced toward one of the grassy ridges that faced away from the mountains. There was mining a few miles beyond that ridge, on land Cade had leased for the purpose. It had been a struggle, that

decision, but in the end he'd bowed to the nation's struggle for fuel independence.

"I wanted to keep the ranch exactly as it was, for my sons to inherit," he said, his voice strangely intense. His eyes searched hers for a long moment. "Do you want children, Abby?"

The question knocked her sideways. She hadn't thought much about children, except when she was around Cade. Now she looked at him and pictured him with a child on his knee, and something inside her burst into wild bloom.

"Yes," she murmured involuntarily.

His gaze dropped lower, to her slender body. "Aren't you afraid of losing your figure?" he asked carelessly, and averted his head while he finished the cigarette.

She didn't dare answer, afraid that her longing for his children would be evident in her voice. Instead, she changed the subject. "Where do you plan to get those sons to leave Painted Ridge to? Are you adopting?"

His dark eyebrows shot up. "I'll get them in the usual way. You do know how people make babies?" he added, a mocking smile shadowing his hard face.

She flushed and turned away. "You always say marriage isn't in your book, Cade. I just wondered, that's all."

"Maybe I'll be forced to change my mind eventually," he remarked, tossing his gloves in the open window of the truck as he followed her back through the trees to the river.

She knelt on one side of the red-checked tablecloth, where she'd laid out foil-covered plates of food and the jug of coffee Calla had packed in the basket.

"Are you going to taste it first?" he asked, moving to the river to slosh water over his face and chest while she dished up the food.

"I think I'll let you, after what you said to her," Abby replied. "She might have put arsenic in it."

"She didn't have time." He came back to the cloth, grabbing up one of several linen towels in the basket. He dabbed at his face and chest, and Abby watched him helplessly, hungrily, as his hands drew the cloth over the warm muscles with their furry covering.

He happened to look up, and his eyes flashed violently at her intense scrutiny.

She couldn't remember a time when she'd felt so intimidated by him or so attracted to him, all at once. She dropped her eyes back to the cloth and dished up the fried chicken, potato salad and rolls, with hands she could barely keep steady.

"Nervous of me, Abby?" he asked quietly, easing his formidable bulk down beside her, far too close, to take the plate she handed him.

"Should I be?" she countered. She poured him a cup of black coffee and automatically added cream before she handed him the Styrofoam cup. "After all, you're the one who should be worrying. I seem to make a habit of throwing myself at you," she added with bitter humor.

"And if you don't get off my ranch pretty quick, Abigail Shane, you may do it once too often," he said flatly. His eyes were dark and full of secrets as he nibbled at a piece of chicken.

"I have utter trust in your remarkable self-control, Mr. McLaren," she muttered, picking at her own food while he put his away like a last meal.

He made a strange sound, a laugh that died away too quickly, and finished his food before he spoke again. He swallowed his coffee and stretched out lazily on the ground while Abby gathered up the remnants of the picnic and put everything except the red-checkered cloth back in the hamper and set it aside.

"You'll be busy with roundup from now on, I guess," she commented after a long silence. Her eyes went to the distant grassy ridges, green and lonely, with pale blue mountains beyond them. The only trees in sight were the ones they were under, and the small thicket of pines nearby. It was like paradise, all clean air and open land and fluffy clouds drifting overhead.

"It's spring," he remarked. "Calves won't brand themselves."

"How's your shoulder?"

"I reckon I won't die," he muttered. He was smoking another cigarette, something he seemed to be doing constantly these days. He had once said it was something he did a lot when he was nervous. That almost made her laugh. He would never be nervous around her.

She drew up her jean-clad legs and rested her chin on her updrawn knees, sighing as she watched the river flow lazily by. "Remember when we came fishing up here the summer I graduated from high school?" she said. "You and me and Melly and a couple of the hands? You caught the biggest crappie I'd ever seen, and Melly got her hook caught in one of the cowboy's jeans. . . ." She laughed, remembering the incident as if it were yesterday.

She stared at the river, lost in memory. It had been a day much like this one. Green and full of sun and

laughter. Hank had been along; so had a cowboy whose name she couldn't remember—one Melly had a crush on. But Abby had somehow wandered close to Cade and stayed there while they fished in the river.

It was just a few weeks after he'd taken her to his room, and she'd been much too shy to approach him, but she'd eased as close as she could get.

"Cold?" he'd teased, glancing down at her.

And she'd blushed, looking away. "Oh, maybe a little," she'd lied. But they both knew the truth, although it didn't seem to bother him a bit.

"Jesse said you'd been thinking about going to New York," he'd mentioned.

"One of my teachers said I had the right carriage and figure and face for it," Abby had said enthusiastically, dreaming how it would be to have Cade and a career all at once.

"New York is a long way from Painted Ridge," he'd murmured, scowling at his fishing rod. "And full of disappointment."

That had pricked her temper, as if he didn't think she were pretty enough or poised enough for such a career in a big city.

"You don't think I can do it?" she'd asked with deceptive softness.

He'd laughed. "You're just a kid, Abby."

"I was eighteen last month. I'm a woman," she'd argued.

His head had turned. His dark eyes had gone over every inch of the shorts and tank top she wore, darkening at the sight of her slender, well-proportioned body.

"You're a woman, all right," he'd said, and looked up.

Her eyes had met his at point-blank range. Even now, she could remember the wild feelings that look had stirred, the hot pleasure of his eyes holding hers. Oblivious to everything around them, she'd actually moved toward him.

And Melly had said something to break the delicate spell. For the rest of the afternoon, they'd fished, and Cade's manner had relaxed a little. She'd tossed a worm at him out of pique when he caught the fish she'd been trying to land for several hours. And he'd picked her up bodily and thrown her in the river. . . .

"You threw me in the river," she remarked suddenly, glaring at him.

His eyebrows arched. "I what?"

"That day we went fishing, the month before I left for New York," she reminded him. "You threw me in the river."

He chuckled softly. "So I did. But you started it, honey. That damned worm hit me right between the eyes."

"It was my fish you caught," she muttered. "My big crappie. I'd half hooked him and he'd gotten away three times. And you just sat there and hauled him out of circulation forever."

"I let you have half of him when Calla cooked him," he reminded her. "That should have made up for it a little."

Her full lips pouted. "I don't know about your half, but mine tasted bitter."

"Sour grapes," he said, grinning. "If you'd caught

him, your half would have been twice as good as mine, wouldn't it?"

She shrugged. "Well, I guess so." Her eyes gazed over the river dreamily. "I used to love fishing. Now I don't have time for anything except work. Or didn't have, until I came back here. Funny how time seems to stop in a place like this," she added quietly. "Not another soul in sight, and you can drive for miles without seeing a ranch house or a store. It must have looked like this when the first settlers came and put down roots. The winter killed a lot of them, didn't it?"

He nodded. "Montana winters are rough. I know. I lose cattle every year, and once we lost a man in a line cabin. He froze to death sitting up."

She shivered. "I remember. That was when I was just out of grammar school. When Melly and I went riding, we wouldn't go near that cabin, thinking it was haunted."

He shook his head. "Well, I've got a couple of old hands now who feel the same way. Hank's one."

"I didn't think Hank was afraid of anything."

He lifted an amused eyebrow. "Do you ever miss this, in New York?"

She searched his face, thinking how she missed him every waking moment. She looked away. "I miss it a lot. There's so much history here. So much privacy and peace." She remembered the role she had to play, almost too late. "But, of course, New York has its good points as well. There's always a new play to see. Sometimes I go to the opera or the ballet. And there are nightclubs and little coffee houses, and museums. . . ."

"None of which you find around here," he said

harshly. "There's not much place for sophistication in the middle of a cattle spread, is there?"

He was watching her with narrowed, calculating eyes, and a dark kind of pain washed over his face before she saw it. Deliberately he crushed out the cigarette on the ground beside him.

She turned, glancing down at him. He was lying on his back with his hands under his head, and his eyes were closed. His powerful legs were crossed, stretching the denim sensuously over their muscular contours. Her eyes took in every detail, from head to broad chest to quiet face, and she felt suddenly reckless.

She picked up a long blade of grass and moved close enough to draw it lightly over his chest.

He grabbed it. "Courting trouble, Abby?" he asked curtly.

There was a wildness in her that sprang from looking at his impassive face. He wouldn't let her close—he spent his life pushing her away. Today would be the last day she'd ever have with him to remember, and today she was going to make him feel something. Even if it was only rage.

"Oh, I just live for it, Cade," she murmured, edging closer. She bent over him before he could stop her, and pressed her lips down on his broad, warm chest.

"God!" he burst out, catching the back of her head. But his hands hesitated, as if he couldn't decide whether to push or pull.

Her nostrils tickled where the thick, curling hair brushed them and she smelled the faint traces of soap and cologne that clung to him. His chest rose and fell with ragged irregularity and she felt the powerful

muscles stiffen as she drew her mouth across them, acting on pure instinct alone.

"You sweet little fool," he rasped. "Oh, God, I'm only human, and I want you until I can hardly stand up straight . . . !"

He jerked her alongside him and bent over her with hands that trembled as his mouth homed in on hers.

Hungry as she'd never imagined she could be, she turned in his big arms and pressed close, half shocked to find his body blatantly aroused as it touched hers. For an instant she tried to draw away, but one lean, steely hand slid quickly to the base of her spine and gathered her hips back against his.

"You wanted it," he ground out against her mouth. "Don't start fighting me now."

Her hands were tangled in the hair over his chest, but she was still rational enough to realize just how involved he already was. "Cade, I only wanted—" she began, only to have the words crushed under his devouring mouth.

"This is what I've been trying to tell you all along," he whispered shakily, moving his lips to her throat. "I want you, Abby. I'd die to have you! And you can feel how much now, can't you? This is how it is between lovers; this is what happens to a man when he's pushed beyond his limits."

Even as he spoke, his hands were sliding under her blouse, finding bare skin at her back and a clasp that snapped apart with devastating ease.

"I haven't been with a woman for so damned long, I'd forgotten how soft . . ." he murmured, sliding his fingers under her breasts to cup their tender weight.

His thumbs found suddenly hard peaks, making her shudder with new pleasure.

Abby's legs moved restlessly as Cade's eased between them. He turned, and she felt the ground under her and the full weight of his big body over her. She moaned at the intimacy, unfamiliar and arousing.

Her sharp nails dug into his back and raked down to his waist, feeling the warmth and moistness of his flesh as his hands touched her in ways that should have shocked her. His mouth was hungrier than she would ever have believed possible. She opened her own mouth helplessly, eagerly, tasting him, experiencing him.

She felt his hands on the buttons of her blouse, and seconds later his chest crushed the softness of her breasts in a joining that made her cry out again.

He lifted his head and his eyes glittered frighteningly. He was trembling all over with desire, and his face was hard with it.

"Is this what you wanted to know?" he demanded unsteadily. "If you could drive me out of my mind with wanting? To see how it would be if you pushed too hard? I want you, all right. I wanted you when you were eighteen, I'd have killed for you. But when I'd made up my mind to ask you to stay with me, you got on that damned bus and you never looked at me!"

Her eyes widened with shock. "What?"

He searched her face with eyes that barely saw. "Every vacation, all I heard about was how great New York was, how well you were doing in your damned career. Until finally I made sure I was out of the house

when you came to visit, because it hurt so much to hear how happy you were away from me."

"But, I wasn't . . ." she began.

He wasn't listening. His hands slid under her hips and forced her up against his. "Feel it, damn you," he whispered harshly. "You've done this to me since you were fifteen. But it's something I hate, Abby, and I hate you, too, for doing it to me, for teasing me. Because I know you don't give a damn for anything except your career and your city men. And nothing you say is going to convince me otherwise!"

She swallowed nervously, her mouth trembling as she realized how set his mind really was. He'd cared, and she hadn't known. Even when Melly told her, she had refused to believe. What had she done?

"Cade," she whispered, reaching a hand up to his face.

"What do you want, baby, to see how I make love? To get a taste of what you missed when you stepped onto that bus four years ago?" He jerked her closer and bent his head. "I don't mind showing you. It will be something to tell your sophisticated friends about when you get back to your own world!" He kissed her again, hurting her, as if it didn't matter anymore whether he hurt her.

She could hardly believe what she'd just heard. He'd cared, he'd really cared enough to ask her not to leave Painted Ridge. And because she'd put on a brave front and gone away laughing, he'd believed it was because she was glad to be leaving him. Of all the horrible ironies . . .

She went limp in his arms, tears washing her face while he treated her like something he'd bought for

the night, his hands insulting, his mouth probing mercilessly into hers. It didn't matter that she loved him more than life, because if she told him now, he wouldn't believe her. He'd just said so, and he thought she was only teasing, playing games with him until she went home. Home. If only he knew that Painted Ridge would always be home—because it was where he was.

She felt cold to the bone, as though there were not a trace of warmth anywhere inside her trembling body. She felt the restless motion of his body against hers, and wondered through a fog of misery if he really meant to take her completely.

But seconds later, he lifted his head as if he'd just tasted the tears, and looked down at her. His face was haunted-looking, his eyes blazing with frustrated passion. His powerful body shuddered.

"And this is as far as it goes, honey," he said with a cold, mocking smile. "You wouldn't want to risk going back to New York with my child growing inside you, would you, Abby? That would be taking the game too far."

Her face felt tight with hurt. She could feel her body trembling under the hard pressure of his, but he'd never know it was with helpless desire, not fear. Despite everything—even his harsh treatment—she still wanted him, would always want him. Nor did the thought of a child bring any terror to her. It was the very door of heaven.

He took a deep breath and rolled away from her, lying with his eyes closed and his bare chest lifting and falling unevenly while she fumbled with catches and buttons.

She got jerkily to her feet and smoothed down her wild blond hair, trying to find the hairpins his insistent fingers had removed. She leaned against one of the sturdy trees by the riverbank until she could get her breath back and stop crying. Finally, she dragged the hem of her blouse over her red eyes to remove the hot, salty tears from her cheeks.

She heard a sound behind her, over the noise of the river washing lazily between the banks, and she knew Cade was standing behind her. But she didn't turn.

"Are you all right?" he asked after a minute, and the words sounded torn from him.

She looked over her shoulder at him, and her ravaged face caused something violent to flash in his eyes.

"Don't look so worried, Cade," she said with enormous dignity. "You made your point. I'm through throwing myself at you. You've cured me for good this time." She managed a soft little laugh, although her swollen lips trembled and spoiled the effect.

He rammed his hands in his pockets and stared at her stiff back. "I'll keep out of your way until Melly gets back from the honeymoon," he said curtly. "I'll expect the same courtesy from you. What happened . . . almost happened here isn't going to be allowed to happen again."

She bit her lower lip to keep from crying. "Cade . . . what you said . . . were you really going to ask me to stay, when I was eighteen?" she asked in a ghost of a whisper.

He laughed bitterly. "Sure," he said. "I was going to offer you the job I finally gave Melly." He looked

away so that she wouldn't see the lie in his dark eyes, or the deep pain that accompanied it.

She straightened, a surge of disappointment and hurt raging through her body. She had hoped that he'd wanted to marry her.

"Can we go back now?" she asked in a subdued tone.

"Might as well. I've got cattle to work."

"And I've got a wedding dress to finish." The sound of her words made her want to scream with anguish. There would never be a wedding for her. She walked quietly to the truck without looking at him and got in.

He loaded the basket and the cloth in the back of the truck with quick, furious motions and paused to shrug into his shirt and slam his ranch hat on his head before he got in beside her.

She felt his eyes on her, but she was staring out at the landscape.

"Abby," he said quietly, "it's better this way. You'll hate me for a while, but you'll get over it."

"I don't hate you," she said in a whisper. "You don't want commitment any more than I do, Cade, so there's nothing to regret."

His hands gripped the steering wheel until his fingers went white. "Don't make it any harder than it already is," he said under his breath. "Let's forget today ever happened, Abby."

"That suits me," she said. She stared out the window as he started the truck and gunned it back onto the road. She wasn't going to cry, she wasn't. She'd thrown her pride at his feet once too often already. He couldn't wait to be rid of her, and she was just as anxious to get away from him. The torment of

loving him was too much. As far as he was concerned, she was just a city girl amusing herself by playing up to him, and nothing was going to convince him otherwise. What a horrible opinion he had of her. Only a man who thought her utterly contemptible could have treated her as he had.

She drew in a shaky breath. It had been so beautiful at first, feeling the hunger raging in him, knowing that he wanted her that much. Until he told her what he really thought, and she realized that it was only physical desire with him after all. Why hadn't she remembered what he'd said the night before about sex being a lousy foundation for a relationship? Well, she remembered now, and she wouldn't forget again. She'd harden her heart and grit her teeth and pray that the three weeks left would go by in a rush. Cade would never get close enough to hurt her again. She was going to make sure of that.

10

Melly's wedding day was a flurry of last-minute preparation, with caterers all over the house and wedding guests arriving in droves even as Abby was helping her sister get into the wedding gown she'd designed.

"It's just heaven." Melly sighed, looking at herself in the mirror. The dress had a keyhole neckline, and it was lavishly trimmed with appliquéd Venice lace. The veil of illusion net that went with it fell from a Juliet cap down to drape over an elegant train. The sleeves were pure lace, the skirt a fantasy of satin and chiffon and more lace, and the Empire waistline featured a row of the most intricate tiny roses in contrasting oyster white. With Melly's blond hair and fair skin, it was sheer magic.

"I can't believe I actually finished it on time," Abby murmured as she made a last tuck in the hem.

"I can't believe you actually designed it," her sister replied. "Abby, it's the most gorgeous thing! Jessica will just die."

"I hope not," came the amused reply. Abby sighed, thinking about what might have been. She'd have to refuse that attractive offer now. It would only have worked if she had stayed in Montana. And, of course, that was impossible. Cade had done everything but move away to keep the distance between them. He wasn't ever at home now, finding excuse after excuse to be up with the dawn and out until bedtime. Sometimes he even camped out with the men in the line cabins, shocking Calla, who gave up on keeping his supper for him and started sending his meals up with Jeb and the boys.

"Melly, be happy," she said suddenly, breaking out of her reverie.

Melly turned, her eyes sparkling and full of love and excitement, her hands trembling with anticipation. "How could I help but be, when I'm marrying Jerry?" she asked. Her joy faded slightly though, when she looked at Abby. "Darling, what's gone wrong between you and Cade?"

"Nothing that hasn't always been wrong," she replied with a cool smile. "Don't you worry about me on your wedding day! Let's get you married, okay?"

"Are you sure you can cope with the computer and all the extra work?"

"I can cope," Abby said quietly. Impulsively, she hugged Melly. "I want years and years of happiness for you. I only wish our parents could be here, to see what a beautiful bride you make!"

"Maybe they're watching," came the soft reply.

"Did you see the flowers, Abby? Wasn't it grand of Cade to let us have the wedding here? All those guests . . ."

". . . will probably have the opportunity to take a look at the bulls he's selling while they're on the place," Abby finished with a bitter smile.

"Shame on you," Melly said gently. "You know how generous Cade is."

Abby flushed and turned away. "We see him in different ways, though. I wonder if he'll show up for the ceremony?"

"He's best man—he'll have to." Melly laughed. "Think you can walk down the aisle on his arm without tripping him?"

"I'll fight the temptation, just for you. You'll listen for the music?"

"I'll listen. See you downstairs."

Abby smiled. "See you downstairs."

She walked out into the hall, checking her own long, V-necked lavender gown for spots or wrinkles. It was sleeveless, and her hair was pinned elegantly atop her head. She carried a bouquet of cymbidium orchids, and she was shaking with nerves. This would be her first wedding, and while she was honored to be her sister's maid of honor, she would rather have been an observer. The hardest thing of all was going to be standing beside Cade at that altar.

She went down the stairs and stopped dead when she caught sight of a redheaded Amazon standing in the doorway. Ignoring the ranch wives, some of whom she knew, she made a beeline for the newcomer, knowing instinctively who she was. Cade, watching from the cleared-out living room where the ceremony

would take place, scowled darkly when he saw her bypass the country women to rush to the elegantly dressed newcomer.

"You've got to be Jessica Dane," Abby said immediately.

The towering redhead grinned. "How'd you guess? It was my beaming smile, right?" She laughed, towering over Abby in her three-inch heels. Barefoot, Jessica would have been almost six feet tall. With her red hair and pale skin and big black eyes, she would have drawn eyes anywhere, even without the mink stole and vivid green silk dress she was wearing with matching shoes and bag.

"You must be Abby, then," Jessica said, extending her hand in a firm, warm handshake. "Come on out to my car for a minute, and let me show you what I brought! Have we got time?"

"A few minutes, anyway." Abby laughed. She went out with Jessica without a backward glance, unaware of the dark scowling face watching her.

"These are just some of my lines," Jessica said when they were seated in the Lincoln Continental's comfortable interior, and Abby thumbed through several catalogs, admiring the fashions.

"They're very good," she said finally.

"They could be better, if I had a house designer," Jessica said. "I'm prepared to offer you a percentage of my gross, Abby. I think you could make us both rich. Richer," she corrected, laughing. "You've got some unique designs, if Melly's wardrobe is anything to go by. I'd love to have you do a few sketches, at least, and send them to me."

Despite her haste to get back to New York, Abby was willing to do that. In fact, she and Jessica got so caught up in a discussion of the particulars, they almost missed the opening chords of the organ. It wasn't until Cade shouted from the front porch that Abby clambored out of Jessica's car and rushed up the steps, with the Amazon at her heels.

"If you can spare the time, everyone else is ready to start," Cade said under his breath as she passed him.

"And the sooner this is over, the sooner she'll be back from her honeymoon, which means I can leave," she shot back, glaring up at him.

"Lady, it won't be quick enough to suit me," he returned hotly.

She brushed past him, oblivious to Jessica's puzzled stare, and went right to the doorway of the living room, arriving just as the prelude finished.

Cade joined Jerry at the altar, the two of them such a contrast in their suits—Cade dark and elegant, Jerry blond and obviously uncomfortable. Then the wedding march sounded and Abby gripped her orchids, shooting a glance at the staircase to find Melly waiting there. As she walked between the folding chairs, she discovered that down the aisle Cade was watching every step she made, an expression in his eyes that she couldn't begin to understand.

For one wild instant, Abby pretended that this was her own wedding, that she was giving herself to Cade for all time. It was so delicious a fantasy that she stared at him the whole length of the aisle. He stared back at her, his face momentarily softening, his eyes black and glittering as she went to stand at her place beside the

flowered arch of the altar. His eyes held hers for a long, blazing moment, and her lips parted on a rush of breath as she felt the force of the look all the way to her toes.

Then the organ sounded again, and the spell was broken as Melly came down the aisle in the gorgeous gown, carrying orchids and wildflowers in a unique bouquet.

Melly walked to the altar and stood nervously beside Jerry. The minister, a delightful man with thick glasses and a contagiously happy expression, read the marriage service. Jerry and Melly each read the special wording that they'd prepared for themselves, and they lit one candle together from two separate candles to signify the joining of two people into one. The final words were read. Jerry kissed the bride for so long that some members of the wedding party began to giggle. And all at once it was over and they were running down the aisle together.

Abby kept out of Cade's way at the reception, sitting aside with Jessica while they discussed modeling and clothes and the future of Jessica's boutique.

Then, all too soon, Melly was dressed in her street clothes and the happy couple rushed out the door to start on their honeymoon. Abby kissed them both and wished them well, and stood by while Melly stopped at the car to toss her wedding bouquet. Calla, dressed in gray and looking unusually sedate, caught it and blushed a flaming red—especially when thin old Jeb, suited up in a rare concession to civilization, looked at her and grinned.

Abby was grateful that she hadn't caught it. That

would have been the final thrust of the knife, to feel Cade's sharp eyes on her, seeing the aching hunger she couldn't have hidden from him.

Hours passed before the guests drifted away, and Abby saw Jessica off with a promise to put some sketches in the mail at her earliest opportunity. She liked Jessica very much. And perhaps there was a way for her to accept the job. If she moved to Wyoming, she'd be far enough away that she wouldn't ever have to see Cade again.

Abby changed into a cotton dress with gold patterning that complemented her pinned-up blond hair and sat down at the supper table expecting to eat alone. It was a surprise when Cade walked into the dining room, wearing a white shirt and blue blazer with dark slacks. He looked impossibly handsome, and as elegant as anything New York might produce.

"Ain't we pretty, though?" Calla murmured, eyeing him as she began to serve the food.

"We shore is," he returned, pursing his lips at her gray dress, which she hadn't changed. "I noticed the way Jeb was looking at you." His eyes narrowed. "Did you bake me another cherry cake and give it to him again?"

The older woman flushed and scowled all at once. "You hush, or I'll burn your supper. You know I gave him the cake on account of he bailed me out when I burned the supper I was cooking for those ranchers you invited here! And what are you doing back here with roundup in full swing? I thought you'd be heading for the hills the minute the words were spoke."

"I live here," he reminded her.

"Could have fooled me," she muttered, waddling out of the room.

Abby fixed her coffee and kept her eyes on her plate. She was still smarting from the ugly remark Cade had made earlier.

"Since we're not speaking, shall I ask Calla to ask you to pass me the salt?" Cade asked coolly.

She handed it over, setting it down before he could take it from her.

"Who was the redheaded Amazon you couldn't part company with?" he asked.

She didn't like the bite in his tone, but it was none of his business who Jessica was. "Another model," she lied, staring at him.

His face hardened. "A successful one, judging by that mink and the Lincoln," he remarked. He smiled bitterly. "Or is she being kept by some man?"

Abby slammed her napkin down by her plate and got up. "Eat by yourself. I can't stand any more of your self-righteousness!"

"You can't stand ordinary people, either, can you?" he challenged. "You walked right past Essie Johnson, and you grew up with her. She wasn't good enough for your exalted company, no doubt, being a simple rancher's wife and all."

That cut to the quick. How could he think her so heartless when in fact she'd gone out of her way to find Essie at the reception and had apologized for what might have appeared to be a snub?

"Think what you like—you will anyway," she said and walked out of the room.

During the week that followed, Cade made himself

scarce. Abby spent her lonely days answering correspondence, putting records into the computer, ordering supplies and answering the phone. If she'd had any hopes that Cade might decide to ask her to stay, they were destroyed by his very indifference. He didn't seem to care whether she spoke to him or not, and while he was courteous, he wasn't the friendly, teasing man of happier times.

The Thursday night before Melly and Jerry were due back on Friday, Abby wandered out by the swimming pool, lost in memory.

Her eyes narrowed on the bare concrete—it was still too early in the year to fill the pool, so it was empty. It seemed a hundred years ago that she'd defiantly stripped off her clothes and gone swimming in it, a lifetime since Cade had found her here half-nude. She'd been hopeful then. She'd had dreams of sharing more than a bed with him. But he'd gently pushed her away. And he hadn't let her come close again, except briefly and physically.

"Remembering, Abby?" Cade asked quietly, coming up behind her from the house.

He was wearing slacks and a burgundy knit shirt that made him look darker and more formidable than ever. His hair was damp, as if he'd showered, and he made Abby's heart race.

She glanced away from his probing gaze. "I was just getting some air, Cade," she murmured.

"The kids come home tomorrow," he remarked carelessly, although the look in his eyes was anything but careless. "I suppose you'll be leaving shortly?"

That hurt. It was as though he couldn't wait to be rid

of her, and she felt the hot threat of tears. She shrugged. "I have commitments. I told you that when I first got here."

He nodded. He held a smoking cigarette in his hand, but he gave it a hard glare and tossed it to the ground and crushed it under his boot.

"You smoke too much," she observed.

He laughed shortly. "I know. I hate the damned things, but it's a habit of long standing."

Like pushing me away, she thought, but didn't speak. Her eyes scanned the starry sky and she wrapped her arms tight around the little blue dress she was wearing.

"Cold, honey?" he asked gently.

She shook her head. "Not very. Calla and Jeb have gone to a movie," she said for no reason.

"And that means that we're alone in the house, doesn't it?" he said. His eyes narrowed. "What do you want me to do about it, Abby, carry you up those stairs to my bedroom, the way I did once before?" He laughed bitterly. "Sorry, honey, I stopped giving lessons that day by the river. Maybe you can find somebody in New York to take over where I left off."

It was like being cut to pieces. "Maybe I can," she said in a taut voice. She turned. "It's late. I'd better go in."

He caught her arm hesitantly, and that puzzled her. He didn't pull her closer, but held her just at his side. "Were you hoping I might come out here?"

She had been, but she would have died rather than admit it now. "I told you before, I'm through throwing myself at your feet, Cade," she replied calmly. "Don't

worry, you're perfectly safe. You can always lock your bedroom door, can't you?"

"Stop that. It's nothing to joke about."

"I wasn't joking." She tugged her arm free. "Good-night, Cade."

"Talk to me, damn it!" he burst out.

"About what?" she shot back. "About my bad manners, my sickening career or my loose morals, all of which you seem to think I enjoy!"

He stiffened. "I've never accused you of having loose morals."

"Except when I come anywhere near you," she said with a bitter laugh.

"You won't try to see my side of it," he ground out. "You're just playing games, but I'm not. I'm too old for it."

"Excuse me, grandpa, I'll try not to unsettle you . . . Cade!"

He jerked her against him and his hands hurt where they gripped her arms. "I want you," he said under his breath. "Don't tempt me. I'm very nearly at the end of my patience as it is. I want you away from Painted Ridge before I do something I don't want to do."

Her lips trembled. "You think I'd let you?" she whispered.

His eyes met hers. "I know you would, and so do you. We go off like dynamite when we start touching each other." His hands dropped. "But it isn't enough. I want more than a feverish night of physical satisfaction. You'd give me that, and I'd give it back. But it's nothing I couldn't have from any of a dozen women,"

he added coldly. "And it's not going to happen—if you get out of here in time."

It was a warning that she was willing to heed. A night with Cade would make it impossible for her to live without him, and she was wise enough to realize it. She dropped her eyes.

"I'll arrange to go Saturday morning," she said.

His face hardened at her subdued tone, but he only nodded. "It's for the best. You came to me hurt, and I hope I've helped you to heal. But your world isn't mine. The longer you stay, the harder it gets. . . ."

He didn't finish it. Instead he lit another cigarette. "You'd better go in. It is getting cold out here."

"Arctic," she mused, glancing up at him. She gathered her poise and her pride and smiled grimly as she brushed past him and went back inside. She moved quickly, grateful that he couldn't see the tears that slid down her cheeks as she went up the stairs. They made her oblivious to the dark eyes that followed her almost worshipfully until she was out of sight.

Melly and Jerry came home looking tanned and rested from their Florida vacation and blissfully happy with each other. Abby could hardly bear their happiness, since it reminded her so graphically that she'd lost every chance of having any of her own with Cade.

"How's everything going here?" Melly asked when they were alone, Jerry having ridden up into the hills to help with roundup.

"Just fine," Abby lied, "but I've had a call from my agency and there's a possibility of a long-term contract for a bottling company. I'm terribly excited about it."

Melly's face fell. "You're going back to New York? But I thought . . . ?"

"Now that you're home, I can leave it all in your capable hands," Abby said with a forced smile. "I've missed New York, and it will be great to get back to work."

"But the attack, the reason you came here . . ."

"Cade helped me over it," Abby said quietly. "I'll always be grateful to him for that. But he wants no part of me—he's made that quite clear. I'm going to do him a favor and go away."

"He loves you, you stupid idiot!" Melly burst out.

Abby flinched and tears welled up in her eyes. "No!" she said huskily. "If he feels anything, it's anger because I preferred modeling to ranch life."

"Have you talked to him, at least?"

"Sure," Abby agreed, not adding that they'd argued every second they were together. "We've both agreed that I have no place in his life, or he in mine." She turned around and walked toward the stairs. "I'm going to pack. Want to help me? I've made reservations on a plane in the morning."

"Oh, Abby, don't do it!" Melly pleaded.

But all her pleading and all her reasoning didn't sway her stubborn sister. The next morning Cade drove the two women out to the airport.

It had been a shock to find him at the wheel of the big sedan when it pulled up at the front door. He was wearing the same navy blazer and dark slacks he'd worn the other night at supper, but he had a striped blue tie over his white silk shirt. The only Western thing about him was his dressy cream Stetson and leather boots.

Her flight was being called as they walked into the terminal, and Abby hugged Melly quickly, suitcase in hand, before she boarded the plane. Tears welled up in her eyes.

"Write to me," she pleaded.

"I will," Melly promised. Her eyes narrowed. "I wish you wouldn't go."

"I have to. I have commitments." She told the lie with panache and a faint smile.

Cade didn't say a word. He stood looking down at her with eyes so dark they seemed black, a smoking cigarette in one hand, his face like flint.

Abby forced herself to look up at him. She was wearing shoes with only tiny heels, and he was taller than ever. Bigger. The most impossibly handsome man she'd ever known, and her heart ached just at the sight of him.

"Bye, Cade," she said quietly. "Thanks for letting me stay so long."

He only nodded. His chest rose and fell heavily, quickly, and his lips were set in a thin line.

"Well . . . I'd better go," Abby said in a high-pitched tone.

Cade threw the cigarette into one of the sand-filled ashtrays and abruptly reached for Abby, crushing her against the length of his body. The suitcase fell and she struggled helplessly for a moment, until he subdued her with nothing more than his firm hold.

She stared into his fierce eyes and stopped fighting, and they looked at each other in a tense, painful exchange that made Abby's knees feel as though they would fold under her. Her lips parted on a sobbing breath, and he bent his head.

It was like no kiss they'd ever shared. His mouth eased down over hers so softly she hardly felt it, and then it moved harder and deeper and slower and rougher until she moaned and reached up, clinging to his neck. He lifted her against him, still increasing the pressure of his arms, his mouth, until she felt as if they were burning into each other, fusing a bond nothing would ever sever. She wanted him. She wanted him! Her mouth, her body, her aching moan told him so, and she could feel the tremor of his own body as the kiss went on and on.

Finally, slowly, he eased her back down onto the floor and breath by breath took his mouth away. His arms slackened and withdrew, although his steely hands held her until she was steady again.

His eyes searched hers. "Goodbye, Abby," he said in a voice like steel.

"Goodbye, Cade," she whispered brokenly.

He brushed his fingers against her cheek, unsteady fingers that touched her as if she'd already become a beautiful illusion. "My God, how I could have loved you!" he breathed. And then, before she could believe her own ears, he turned and strode quietly away, without once looking back.

Abby stared after him, uncomprehending. "Did . . . did I just hear what I thought I heard?" she murmured.

"What, honey?" Melly asked gently, coming back within earshot. "I was being discreet. Gosh, what a kiss that was! And you're leaving?"

Abby sighed bitterly. Surely she'd dreamed it, or misunderstood . . . or had she? She took a steadying breath. "I have to go. I'll miss my flight. Melly, take care of him?"

"You could have done that yourself, if you'd told him the truth," Melly said softly. "It's still not too late. You could catch him."

"He wouldn't listen," she said wearily. "You know how Cade is when he makes up his mind, and I've gone mad and started hearing things again. Back to the salt mines, Melly. I'm fine now, I'm just fine. Take care. I love you."

"I love you, too." She searched her sister's eyes. "He couldn't have kissed you that way without caring one hell of a lot. Think about that. Hurry now!"

Abby waved and ran for the plane. And all the way back to New York she thought and thought about that long, hard kiss and what she imagined Cade had said until she all but went crazy. Finally, in desperation, she tucked the memory in the back of her mind and closed her eyes. It was over now; he'd sent her away. Looking back was no good at all. She'd had time to recuperate and get herself back together. Now she had to put Montana and Cade behind her and start over. She could do it. After all, her career was all she had left.

11

It took several days for Abby to adjust to city life again after the wide-open country of Montana. Accustomed to staying up late at the ranch, she now had to go to bed early, watch her diet, be concerned with shadows and lines of weariness, add to her wardrobe and pack her huge handbag with the dozens of items she might need for an assignment. And every night she soaked her aching feet and smothered herself in cold cream and longed for Cade McLaren with every cell in her body.

She did Jessica's sketches in the weeks that followed and mailed them to Wyoming. Jessica phoned her shortly afterwards and invited her out to see the boutique, but Abby had to put her off. She was working feverishly, and the lie she'd told Melly about the bottling company commercials had been amazingly prophetic. She was offered a television commercial

for a soft drink company, which she immediately accepted. Her career was skyrocketing. And it was as empty as her life.

She didn't even bother dating other men. What was the use, when all she could do was compare them to Cade. So she worked and grieved for him, and before very long the toll of loneliness began to show on her.

All the years before, she'd had that sweet memory of him to sustain her, and the hope that someday things might change. But now there was no hope left. There was nothing to cling to, only a future that was empty and lonely. Even if she accepted Jessica's offer and went to live in Wyoming, she might be near Cade but she'd still be alone. She didn't know how she was going to bear it.

Late one Friday night, she was halfheartedly watching television when the phone rang. She couldn't imagine who it could be at that hour, and she was frowning when she picked up the receiver.

"Hello?" she murmured.

"Hello, honey," came a deep, painfully familiar voice. She sat down, paling. It had been almost four months since she'd last heard that particular voice, but she would have known it on her deathbed.

"Cade?" she whispered shakily.

"Yes." There was a pause. "How are you, Abby?"

She drew in a slow breath. Don't panic, she told herself, don't give yourself away. "I'm just fine, Cade," she said brightly.

"No date on a Friday night?" he murmured.

She drew her gold caftan closer around her, as if he could see her all the way from Montana. "I was tired," she replied. "Is everything all right? Melly . . . ?"

"Melly's fine. She and Jerry are down at Yellowstone for the weekend."

"Oh." She gripped the receiver tightly. "Then nothing's wrong?"

"Everything's wrong," he said after a minute. "Hank's quitting."

"Hank!" She sat straight up. "Why?"

He laughed mirthlessly. "He says I'm too damned mean to stay around."

"Are you?" she asked softly. There was something strange about his voice, different. "Cade, are you all right?" she asked, and the concern seeped through.

"I'm . . . fine." He laughed again. "I'll be finer when I get through this bottle."

"You're drinking!" It was the only thing that could explain the way he sounded.

"Are you shocked? I'm human, Abby, although you sure as hell never thought I was, did you?" There was a thud and a muffled curse. "Damn, why does furniture have to sprout legs when you try to go around it?"

She wrapped the telephone cord around her fingers. "Cade, is someone there with you? Calla?"

"Calla's gone to a movie with Jeb. Any day now I expect to be asked to the wedding." He sighed. "Abby, before long you and I are going to be the only two single people on earth."

"Why are you drinking?" she asked, worried. "You haven't gotten hurt, have you?"

"You're a hell of a person to ask me that," he growled. "You cut the heart out of me when you got on that damned plane. Just the way you cut it out when you got on the bus four years ago. Oh, God,

Abby, I miss you!" he ground out, his voice throbbing with emotion. "I miss you!"

Tears burst from her eyes and rolled down her cheeks. "I miss you, too," she whispered. Her eyes closed and she bit her lip. "Every hour of every day."

There was a long, deep sigh from the other end of the line. "We should have made love that day by the river," he said achingly. "Maybe we would have gotten each other out of our systems. I've got a picture of you by my bed, Abby. I sit here and look at it and ache all over."

Her fingers clenched until the blood went out of them. She had one of him, too, that she'd carried to New York with her four years before. It was wrinkled from being hugged against her heart.

"You're the one who told me sex was a bad foundation to build on," she reminded him wearily.

"It wasn't just sex," he said. "It's never been that. Four years ago, I couldn't risk getting you pregnant, don't you see? I couldn't take the choice away from you. To hell with how I felt, I couldn't force you to stay here, Abby."

Her breath caught in her throat. She caught the receiver with both hands and sat as stiff as a poker. Did he even realize what he was admitting?

"You . . . you thought that given the choice between you and modeling . . ."

"You showed me which was more important, didn't you, honey?" he asked with a bitter laugh. He sighed heavily. "You got on that bus, laughing like a freed prisoner, and you never even looked at me. I told your father I'd marry you, if you'd have me, and we fought it out half the night. He said you were too young and

you wanted a chance to get away from the ranch, to be somebody. I argued with him then, but when it came down to it, I couldn't make you stay with me." His voice was faintly slurred, but just as beautiful as ever, and Abby was hurting in ways she'd never dreamed she could. "You see, I'd already realized how vulnerable you were with me. And I was just as vulnerable with you. I had to be careful not to come too close, Abby, because we could have gotten in over our heads. I figured you'd go to New York and get tired of the city and come back to me. But you didn't."

There was a world of emotion in those words. Bitterness. Hopelessness. Hurt.

"You never asked me to stay," she whispered. "You said you didn't want a commitment to any woman, a . . . a leash on your freedom."

He laughed. "I haven't been free since you were fifteen years old. I've never wanted anyone else. I never will."

"You let me go!" she burst out, suddenly hating him. "Damn you, you let me go! I was only eighteen, but there was nothing New York had to offer that could have torn me away from you if you'd just told me to stay! One lousy word, just one word—stay. And you let me go, Cade!"

There was a shocked pause on the other end of the line, a silence like darkness in a graveyard.

But she didn't notice. The words were tumbling out of her, while tears burned down her cheeks. "I loved the glamour, you said, I couldn't live without the city! And all I've done for four years is stare at this picture of you and cry my eyes out! You put me on a bus four years ago, and you put me on a plane four months

ago . . . damn you, what do you care? You push me away, you accuse me of teasing you, you . . . Cade? Cade!"

But the line was dead. She slammed the receiver down and burst into tears. If he called back, she wasn't even going to answer. Let him sit and drown in his whiskey. She didn't care! She turned off the lights and went to bed in a fit of furious temper.

Several hours later, she sat straight up in bed as the doorbell rang and rang and rang. Maybe she was dreaming it. It had taken her forever to get to sleep, and she was still drowsy. She laid her head back on the pillow, but there it came again, even more insistently.

Frowning sleepily, she padded to the front door of her apartment with her gold caftan swirling around her.

"Who is it?" she grumbled.

"Who the hell do you think? Open the door, or do I have to break it down?"

"Cade?" Her heart jumped wildly and she fumbled the catch and the safety latch off and opened the door. And it was no dream.

He came into the apartment with a scowl as black as thunder on his dark face, looking sleepy and tired and worn out. He was wearing jeans and a half-open denim shirt, and old boots and the battered brown ranch hat he wore to work cattle. His boots were dusty, his face needed a shave and he was altogether the most beautiful sight Abby had seen in her life.

"Cade!" she breathed, blinking up at him out of sleepy eyes, her tangled hair glorious in its disarray,

the caftan clinging lovingly and quite revealingly to every line of her body.

"I've had half a bottle of whiskey," he said, towering over her with the locked door behind him. "And I'm not quite sober yet, despite the three cups of black coffee I had on the plane. But you said something to me that I'm sure I really heard and didn't dream, and I flew up here to let you say it again. Just to make sure."

She stared at him unblinkingly, loving every unshaven plane of his face.

"You hung up the phone and got on a plane in the middle of the night . . . ?" she began nervously.

His eyes roamed down her body and one dark eyebrow arched curiously. "You've lost weight, Abigail," he murmured, studying her. "A lot of it, and you look like pure hell."

"Have you seen yourself in a mirror?" she countered, noticing new lines, new shadows under his dark eyes.

He shook his head. "Couldn't stand the sight of myself," he admitted. "Come on, Abby, let's hear it."

She swallowed. "It was easier when you were still in Montana," she began nervously.

"I guess it was." He took off his hat and tossed it onto a chair. His big hands framed her face and he looked down at it like a starving man. "Suppose I take you to bed, Abby?" he asked softly. "And after we've made love for three or four hours, I'll ask you again."

12

She could barely breathe when she saw what was in his eyes. It was hardly possible that she was dreaming, but it was so much like a dream come true that she felt faint.

"Look at me, Abby," he whispered.

She raised her eyes and his gaze fell to the transparent material over her firm, high breasts. He reached out and drew his knuckles down from her collarbone over one perfect breast, and he smiled at her body's helpless reaction to his touch, at the hunger he could see and feel.

"Same damned thing happens to me every time I think about you," he murmured with a soft, deep laugh. "Four months, Abby. Four long months, and I've walked around aching every minute of every day, wanting you until I was like a wounded bear with everyone around me. Tonight I'd had all I could take, I

couldn't even get properly drunk . . . damn you, come here!"

He lifted her in his hard arms, taking her mouth with a hungry, aching thoroughness, ignoring her sweet moan of pleasure and her clinging arms as he walked back into her bedroom and slammed the door behind them.

"I'm going to make love to you all night long," he said as he carried her straight toward the bed. "In the morning, you'll be damned lucky if you can walk at all. Then we'll talk."

"Cade, I could get pregnant!" she said in a high-pitched tone, afraid that it was only the liquor talking.

"Yes, you could," he said quietly, staring into her eyes. "And that would mean total commitment. To me. For life. Say yes or no. But if it's no, I'm going straight back to Montana, and I'll never come near you again."

She felt her body trembling in his strong embrace, and her heart yielded totally as she searched his face with a loving, possessive gaze.

"I don't know if I can survive an affair with you," she said softly. "But if that's what you want, I . . . I can try. I just don't understand what we'd do about a child. . . ."

He breathed slowly, deliberately, and his eyes softened. "Melly said you were blind about me. I suppose she knew better than I did," he murmured. He laid her gently down on the bed and unbuttoned his shirt with slow, easy motions, tossing it aside. His hands went to his belt and unfastened it. His trousers followed, while Abby watched him, shocked to the bone.

"If you think it's rough on you," he muttered, glancing at her as he turned to divest himself of everything else, "remember what I told you before, Abby. I've never undressed in front of a woman."

"That's the loss of women everywhere," she whispered, awed as he turned around again. "Oh, Cade . . . !"

His face softened, and the red stain on his cheeks faded away. He sat down beside her, coaxing her to sit up so that he could remove the caftan. And then he just looked and looked, until she felt her heart trembling wildly, her body helplessly arching in invitation, moving restlessly under the pure sensuality of the appraisal.

"Before this goes any further," he said quietly, sliding a big, warm hand over her smooth belly, up to rest maddeningly below one taut breast, "you'd better tell me if you meant what you said on the phone."

She swallowed. "About being lonely and lost in the city?" she whispered.

He nodded. "Are you happy?"

"When I'm with you," she managed through trembling lips. "Only when I'm with you. Oh, God, you don't know . . . you'll never know how it was to leave you!"

His fingers trembled and he searched for his voice. "I know how it was to be left, Abby," he said slowly. "I've been walking around like half a man for four years. And until tonight, I had no idea, no idea at all what you felt."

"How could I tell you, when you kept going on about not wanting a commitment, not wanting mar-

riage?" she asked unsteadily. "You pushed me away. . . ."

"I had to," he ground out. "I can't control what I feel for you, I never could. You'll never know how close I came to taking you the night I found you by the pool. When I left you I was shaking like a boy. I had to drink myself to sleep—the only other time I've been at the bottle like I have tonight." His fingers moved up to her breasts, touching them like a man touching a treasure trove. "So beautiful," he whispered. "You were then, you are now. My Abby. My own."

Abby's hands reached up and stroked his chest, tickling as they pressed into the tangle of dark hair. "I never knew," she whispered.

"Neither did I." He shuddered as her hands caressed him. "Don't do that, not yet. I go crazy when you touch me that way."

"You said we were going to make love," she reminded him softly.

"We are. When you agree to marry me," he said quietly. "I couldn't handle an affair with you, either. If I take you, you take me for life."

It was important to know the truth, not just guess at it. There had been too much misunderstanding already. "Because you need sons to inherit Painted Ridge?" she asked in a whisper.

"Because I love you, Abigail Shane," he corrected breathlessly. "Because I've loved you for so many years that loving you is a way of life for me. Because if you don't come home with me, I'll pack my bags and move in with you and make love to you until you'll marry me in self-defense, just to get some rest."

Tears welled up in her wide brown eyes as they searched his. "You love me, Cade?" she burst out.

"What a mild word for so much feeling," he managed in a voice that shook. His hands framed her face, and his eyes worshipped it. "I want to be with you all the time. I want to sit and watch you when we're together. I want to stay by your bed when you're sick and you need me. I want to hold you in my arms in bed at night, even when we don't make love. I want to give you children. Most of all, I want to live with you until I die. All the good days and bad. All the way to the grave."

She was crying helplessly at his admission, at having all her wildest dreams come true. Her fingers moved up to his hard face and lovingly traced every warm inch of it. "I couldn't look at you when I got on the bus four years ago," she said brokenly, "because if I had, I would have thrown myself at your feet and begged you to let me stay. I started loving you when I was barely fifteen, and I've loved you every day since. Hopelessly, with all my heart. Oh, God, Cade, it was never New York and modeling. It was you! I love you until I hurt all over! I'll love you all my life, all the days I live . . . !"

He stopped the frantic words with his mouth and eased down beside her. They kissed slowly, sweetly, rocking in each other's warm arms, savoring the newness of belonging to each other, of shared loving. Until his tongue gently penetrated her mouth. Until her lips opened to its deep searching. Until they moved, together, slowly, into a new and shattering kind of intimacy with each other.

"Teach me how, Cade," she whispered with love

splintering her voice as she felt his hands touching her in new ways. "Teach me how . . . to show love . . . this way."

His mouth gentled hers. "We'll learn it together, honey," he whispered back. "Because this is like my first time, too. Tell me if I hurt you. I'd rather die than hurt you now."

But even as he spoke, his mouth was moving against her body, and she forgot that it was the first time, she forgot everything but the glory of being kissed and touched so tenderly by the only man she'd ever loved. She relaxed and moved deliberately, touched deliberately, delighting in his reactions to her fingers, her mouth. She whispered her love; her body shouted it.

Sensation piled on sensation, while she turned and arched and whispered wildly into his ear as he moved against her so slowly, with such staggering control. She could barely believe that the level of pleasure she was experiencing was bearable as it mounted and mounted and began to possess her.

Her eyes opened on a surge of mingled need and fear, and his were open, too, staring back at her.

"Don't be afraid of me," he whispered shakenly, urgently. "I love you. Trust me."

It was all she needed to push her over the edge. Her eyes closed again, and she felt his mouth gentling hers, preparing her for what was coming.

Her hands tangled in his thick, dark hair as his body slowly, tenderly, overwhelmed hers. His mouth was gentle, despite the need she could feel in him, a need he was deliberately denying for her sake. The very tenderness of his movements, his slow, soft kisses,

made it so beautiful that she forgot her fear and gave herself up to the incredible intimacy of belonging to him.

If there was pain, she hardly noticed it, so involved was she in trying to get closer to him, trying to please him as he was pleasing her. She wanted nothing more than the joy of giving everything she had to give.

He cherished her as she'd never dreamed a man could cherish a woman, every second fueling the hunger and the sweetness of sharing love. She clung to him, loving him, loving him! And it was so easy. So perfect. So beautiful. Her eyes burned with tears that rolled helplessly down her cheeks into their joined mouths. A moment later she heard his voice in her ear, whispering words that only vaguely registered, whispering her name like a litany.

And from tenderness came passion—suddenly, like a summer storm billowing over them, lifting and tossing them in a vortex of urgency that blazed brighter than the lights around them.

She heard her voice break, and felt his hands controlling her wild movements firmly, guiding, teaching. Her teeth bit into his hard shoulder in an agony of pleasure, so exquisite that she cried out. And then there was no more time for the gentle beginnings, only for the wild, furious stretch toward fulfillment that sent them crashing together in frantic torment, trembling wildly, whispering urgently until there was oneness. And then peace.

Later, she curled up against him, trembling, while he lit a cigarette and smoked it. She laughed softly, triumphantly, delightedly.

His arm drew her closer, and he chuckled softly,

too. "My God, in all my wildest dreams I never imagined feeling like that."

"Neither did I," she returned. "I thought I'd died."

His chest rose and fell heavily. "I'm going to have that book framed and hung over our bed after we're married."

She blinked. "Book?"

He chuckled wickedly. "There's this book about making love that I bought a few weeks ago," he murmured. He lifted his brows at her stunned expression and laughed uproariously. "Well, hell, Abby, I told you I spent half my life working with the damned cattle. Where did you expect me to learn about sex? You women, always expecting men to know all the answers and hating us for the way we get them. . . ."

Her face brightened with wonder. "Why, you old devil," she said. "And I thought you had a string of women a mile long!"

He kissed her nose. "You're my woman. The only one I ever wanted. I haven't been a monk, but there was never any joy for me in sleeping with women I didn't even like."

She stared up at him curiously. "You mean, you learned everything you just did to me out of a book?!"

His eyebrows arched. "It was a good book," he said defensively, "kind of a primer . . . well, damn it, I thought that after I gave you a while to think about me and the ranch, and maybe miss me, I might come up here and try to change your mind. I was going to wait until Christmas. . . ." He shrugged his powerful shoulders. "Then tonight, after Calla went out with Jeb, I got lonely and started drinking." He sighed. "First time I've put away that much whiskey in years." He

looked down at her radiant face. "When you started ranting and raving at me, it was the sweetest music I'd ever heard. I didn't even take time to shave, I just got Hank out of bed to drive me to the airport."

"You said he was quitting!"

"When he found out I was on my way to you, he took back his resignation," Cade said, grinning. "Told me he had wondered if I planned to stay stupid all my life."

"I think we were both a little dense," she replied. Her eyes devoured him. "I love you," she whispered intensely.

"I love you," he replied, bending to kiss her softly, slowly, with tender promise. "Can you live with me on Painted Ridge and give up all you've accomplished? If not, I'll compromise, now that I know you love me."

"I could give up breathing if you'll make love to me every night," she murmured, pressing close. "I hate it here. After the first few months, all the glamour and adventure wore off. I worked like a zombie all day and dreamed all night about how it would be to sleep in your arms and carry your child in my body. . . ."

He drew in a sharp breath. "Don't say things like that to me, I'll go crazy."

"Take me with you," she said, brushing her hand over his chest and smiling when he trembled. "Let's go together."

"In a minute." He put out the cigarette and leaned over her, his eyes solemn. "I can't expect you to sacrifice four years of hard work just to raise children. I don't want you to give up being a person just because you're my wife. We all need to feel fulfillment, a sense of purpose."

"Oh, my gosh, I didn't ever tell you about Jessica Dane!" she burst out, and explained it all, even her behavior at the reception.

He sighed angrily. "Well, I was a damned fool over that, wasn't I?" he ground out. He kissed her gently. "I'm sorry, honey."

"It's all right. You didn't know." She touched his mouth. "So you see, I could work for Jessica and never leave the house except to supervise some seamstresses once in a while. And I've always preferred designing to modeling, anyway."

"Lucky me," he said. He grinned. "If we have little girls, you can make party dresses for them, too."

She laughed. "Not for the little boys, though. I don't want my sons parading around in petticoats." She leaned forward and kissed him lazily. "My throat's sore from talking. Teach me some more things you learned in that book of yours."

He chuckled. "There's just one more little thing to talk about. I had Hank promise to make a few phone calls for me after daylight."

"Did you?" she murmured, nibbling at his lips.

"I had him invite the minister over for next Saturday."

"That's nice," she whispered. Her hands smoothed over his long, tanned body.

"Plus about fifty other people."

"Ummm," she murmured. Her hands moved to his hair-roughened chest and she pressed against him. "That's nice, too."

"For the wedding."

She drew away. "Next Saturday?!"

"Why wait?" he asked, biting at her mouth. "I sure

was hoping you'd say yes, Abby. All the way here I had nightmares about trying to line up a bride and groom at such short notice if you refused me. . . ."

"Cade Alexander McLaren, what am I going to do with you?" she asked sharply.

"Lie down here and I'll show you," he murmured with a laugh, easing her onto her back. "This is the best chapter of all. . . ."

Abby smiled as she met his hungry mouth. When they got home to Painted Ridge, she had some heavy reading to do.